*Ethel
and the
Naked Spy*

By Marc Lovell

Ethel
and the
Naked Spy

MARC LOVELL

A CRIME CLUB BOOK

DOUBLEDAY

NEW YORK   LONDON   TORONTO   SYDNEY   AUCKLAND

A Crime Club Book
Published by Doubleday, a division of
Bantam Doubleday Dell Publishing Group, Inc.
666 Fifth Avenue, New York, New York 10103

DOUBLEDAY and the portrayal of a man
with a gun are trademarks of
Doubleday, a division of Bantam Doubleday Dell
Publishing Group, Inc.

Library of Congress Cataloging-in-Publication Data

Lovell, Marc.
Ethel and the naked spy / Marc Lovell.
p.   cm.
"A Crime Club book."
I. Title.
PR6062.O853E84   1989
823'.914—dc19   88-8023
CIP

ISBN 0-385-24989-6

*Ethel
and the
Naked Spy*

ONE

The country pension, in an isolated spot beyond the last eastward suburb of Paris, was alive with the activity of a city hotel. Indoors or out on this spring evening people milled and gathered, came and went, bustled. Strangers they greeted with smiling courtesy, mere acquaintances like twins. They clicked cameras at each other. They tried to see everything at once and be everywhere at once, continually looking around, incessantly entering the lobby or going outside. The excitement was powerful enough to catch under a net.

Or so Apple mused as he came into the lobby from his room. He had bathed and changed since his arrival two hours ago, when the scene had been more tranquil. Jeans and sweater, he was glad to note, seemed to be the right kind of uniform, which meant that the glances sent his way were for the usual reason.

Appleton Porter was six feet seven inches tall. This would have been fine if it weren't that, for reasons both social and professional, he yearned to be six one. The extra, unnecessary inches formed the second biggest bane of his life, close behind the first, a penchant for blushing, though it was only his logical side that prevented his top banes from switching places: he would willingly have suffered a blush a day forever in exchange for a height cure, had such a thing been possible. There was, whereas, always hope for a cure for bane one. About bane five, his logical side, he rarely bothered to think.

Apple was not the imposing person his stature could have allowed him to be. In manner he was too diffident, in appearance too bland. His short neat hair was the same ginger shade as the freckles that lay across his paleness like gold coins flung onto a sheet, not to pay for sin but the laundry. With regular features to give no help, only Apple's keen green eyes escaped the bane category, especially when they got together with his mouth to express delight.

Polite interest was what Apple acted as he pushed ahead, penetrating the assembly. The excitement sizzled on. Apple felt excited himself. He still would have felt so, he knew, even if the ambience hadn't been catching. His business here was stirringly serious.

The fifty-odd people who were creating the ambience, they ranged in age from the twenties to around the sixty mark. While their clothing might be casual, in respect of the majority the tones of their British English, their complexions and the way they held their heads told of them being strangers to subservience, free education and fried bread.

Several times as he circulated Apple got stopped by someone in greeting. He was offered a name and a hearty handshake, slapped on the bicep, told he was welcome and rather tall. The ones he himself went out of his way to stop were young and female. He didn't forget the bicep routine, though he inclined more toward pat than slap.

When, now, Apple got stopped again it made his heart twitch. He recognised one of the Possibles.

Enrico Balto, born Sidney Witherspoon, was a

singer. One of Britain's leading operatic tenors, a chesty man of forty-five, he had abundant dark hair to attend his full beard and help a nose with a hook, facially all ready to stride onstage with a buccaneer's aria. He even wore an ear-ring. But the front rows would have seen through his act: pirates don't move their eyes around in hops and flinches; they glare fit to maim.

Exchange of grips and names over, Enrico Balto asked the floor, "You're new, aren't you, Mr. Porter?"

"Yes. This is my first."

"Mine too. And for several others, I believe."

As though he didn't know exactly, Apple said, "There seem to be quite a few recent members, yes."

"New blood," Balto told his elbow dejectedly.

"And famous if not blue."

The opera singer shot up a brief glance. It could have held jealousy or wariness. He said, "Adele Pringle is not all that well known."

"I wasn't referring to Ms. Pringle in particular."

"Dr. Whittington, then. She does, I suppose, possess a certain name in the world of academe."

"So I understand."

Again Enrico Balto did his upstab of a glance at Apple's face, before asking his shoulder, "Are you perhaps celebrated yourself, Mr. Porter?"

"Oh no," Apple said. "Not in the least."

"If so, you must please forgive my ignorance. I know so little of what goes on outside my own world, that of opera. I'm a singer, you see."

"I know, Mr. Balto. I've heard you often and I once nearly got a ticket to see you at Covent Garden."

"Thank you," Enrico Balto said, patting his tank chest. "Your own fame would pass me by, I'm afraid. To me nothing but opera matters."

"I am not a celebrity, Mr. Balto."

"Nothing else is of consequence. Opera is my whole life. You could have been front-page news for weeks and I simply wouldn't know."

Apple said, "Okay."

"You could be a household word, with your name and face familiar to everyone in the realm, and to me —nothing."

Feeling vaguely that he was lying, and lowering his voice, Apple repeated that he was not a celebrity. Enrico Balto rolled over with, "Just as well. Otherwise we might be swamped with media people. Terrible nuisance."

Unaware that he spoke with a tinge of weariness, the pestered star, Apple said, "Oh, I know."

"Fortunately, reporters and such long ago accepted that, unspoilt though I may be by my exceptional talent and worldwide renown, I do draw the line at interviews. I never give them."

"I don't either."

"Sell them, yes," Enrico Balto said. "To periodicals of taste and import. It's all part of the commercial side of one's art. One has to exist."

"I couldn't agree more."

Slapping Apple's bicep while looking the other way, in the direction he was moving off in, the opera singer said they must get together again soon. "You can tell me about those times you saw me at Covent Garden."

"Well . . ."

"Good-bye."

Himself moving on, Apple, to counter a dullness he was feeling at knowing he wasn't famous, recalled that the opera house just named stood in an area that was once the vegetable garden of a convent. When

this had small effect, maybe because he couldn't explain why the first *n* had been dropped, he self-con-
gratulated on his progress: smoothly getting on close
terms with one of the Possibles.

Up again, humming that chirpy bit from *Carmen*,
Apple set about leaving the crowd before his claustrophobia could start to let itself be heard, tapping at
his reason. He went to the main door.

On the huge front step outside, Apple stopped.
The scene had changed from its earlier quiet. The
dirt frontage, bordered inevitably by poplars, was a
jumble of cars and people, some of both on the move.
Horns beeped, voices were raised, engines raced,
laughter rocketed. Although unconfined by walls, the
seethe of excitement was no weaker outdoors than in.

It tickled Apple's scalp as he gazed around, his
height plus the step giving him Big Brother coverage.
An extra tickle ran up from nape to crown as, in the
middle distance, he spotted a woman in a yellow
sweater. He left the step.

Adele Pringle was forty and hefty. She looked no
more like a poet than an orchid looks like a cat. Her
face was square, her features lumpy, her eyes forth-
right. She had brown hair formed like a Nazi helmet,
one that ought to have been on someone with a much
smaller head. The grey streak down the front of her
sweater, yellow because she always wore yellow, had
been caused by cigarette ash.

When Apple arrived beside Adele Pringle, where
she leaned back on the side of an ochre-coloured car,
studying a map, he was in time to see an inch of ash
fall sweaterwards from the cigarette she held in her
lips but not fast enough to catch it.

As the poet flinched at the out-darting hands, Apple was already ending their flight. Dropping them and straightening from his hunch, he said, "Sorry." She asked, "What?" He said, "Never mind."

Adele Pringle lowered her map. Speaking around the cigarette, she said, "Can I help you?"

"I'm new. I thought I should introduce myself."

"Brave of you. I'm hopeless at all the social stuff. My name's Adele Pringle. How do you do."

"How do you do. Appleton Porter. Friends call me Apple."

"How sweet. Mine call me Pring. Never been sure whether I like it or not. Suppose I must. I'll have to give it a think one of these days."

They nodded at each other. Apple said, "I must confess I've never read any of your poetry."

"Millions haven't, dear."

"You're highly praised by the critics."

"And unknown to the public," Adele Pringle said. "But as I don't need to earn my bread from scribbling, I'm not precisely shattered." She coughed her cigarette end out and trod on it. "You're not a poet yourself or anything awful like that, are you, dear?"

"Philology's my game," Apple said, adding a casual, "Pring."

"You're coming along as an interpreter?"

"No, a member, but I'll be able to step into breaches, if need be."

While bringing out a pack of cigarettes, Adele Pringle asked how many languages he spoke. Since the truth always made him seem a braggart, in Apple's view, he reduced the tally: "Oh, seven or so."

"That's about the number of words I know in French. And they're all disreputable."

Apple told the poet she would no doubt survive

and she said, tapping the map against the car at her back, "Roderick's all I need."

"That's how I feel about Ethel," Apple said.

Mainly pale green, she had a centre stripe of orange and wheels of brothel red. The paint job would have quirked not an eyebrow had it garnished a beach buggy, but, being on an old London taxi, it did tend to unnerve radicals and swell the traditionalist with outrage.

Apple thought Ethel beautiful. He turned back to look at her on that grey morning, in that grey East End street, feeling the pride whose major portion he had never recognised as being for his courage. Nor did he, arch-conservative dresser that he was, know he not so much drove Ethel as wore her.

Apple went on. Nervously he told himself not to be nervous. Everything was going to be o-very-kay. This was sure to be a bit of work, probably on a team, and the more insouciant he acted the stronger would be Angus Watkin's wish to employ him. Nothing incites people's interest in a person more than that person's indifference.

Which adage plus a thousand others Apple had learned years before at Damian House, the country mansion where he had been trained in the wiles and wherefores of espionage. It was the only course in which he hadn't scored near the bottom of his group. However, aided by 10s in Languages and Security Clearance, an examiner away sick and a girl in the office who liked his eyes, he had managed to scrape through to acceptance.

Since that time, while working as a senior official at the United Kingdom Philological Institute, Apple had been used in the field but rarely by his depart-

ment, called Upstairs, a branch of British Intelligence. This neglect, Apple preferred to believe, was
due to his being so tall, which made blending into the
human scenery difficult. Deep down he knew his
height was only one of those Drawbacks cruelly
listed in his dossier:

Porter is subject to blushing. Is sentimental by nature. Has a fondness for collecting useless information. Is a poor drinker. Has a dislike of violence and
an aversion to firearms. Is apt to fall in love on the
slimmest provocation.

Even so, there had been times when Angus Watkin,
his Control, who regularly used him for drab lan-
guage-related tasks, had actually sent Apple out on a
mission. Afterwards, he had never said thank you.

Smoothing his dull suit, twitching the knot of his
tedious tie, Apple went into the rendezvous. The ad-
dress of the workers' café had been given him by telephone an hour ago at his flat in Bloomsbury, the unknown informant ending, "Be there on the stroke of
ten."

Counter deserted, the only person present, now
that the breakfast rush had passed, was a man sitting
at one of the unpainted tables. They were well suited,
table and man, although Angus Watkin would have
looked equally at home in a banquette at the Ritz. He
was that type.

Middle-aged and colourless, plainly dressed, the
spymaster would take on the characteristics of his
surroundings, looking seedy down an alley yet sedate
in a bank, sinister in a dive yet amiable by a hearth,
moronic up a tree yet wise behind an opulent desk.

At the moment he could have passed as a bookmak-
er's clerk or an unemployed waiter, though there was
something of the sanitary inspector in the way he

looked into his cup while saying, "Bolt the door and sit here, Porter."

"Good morning, sir," Apple said when he had obeyed. "It's a fine day."

"Apart from the cold and damp."

"Exactly, sir."

"Unpleasant."

"Could be brighter, yes."

Pushing his cup aside Angus Watkin looked up pallidly. There was no sign that he had enjoyed his usual ploy of reminding the underling of his place. He said:

"But I didn't ask you to come here to have a chat about the weather. Please attend."

Displaying contrition: "Sorry, sir. Yes, sir."

"I believe you own, Porter, a vehicle of a certain age."

Apple knew that Watkin knew that Apple knew of Ethel's being known to Watkin, who, indeed, had been aware of her existence long before her present owner had. Until being retired for looking too old to pass as a working taxi, she had been operated by various law-enforcement agencies, including Upstairs.

Nevertheless, Apple said, "As a matter of fact, sir, I do." He blinked as if with admiration.

"And it is over forty years old?"

"She certainly is."

Angus Watkin said, "Then allow me to tell you about BOVA, which stands for British Old Vehicles Association. Or rather, tell you about the club's annual rally. But perhaps you know of it already."

Even if he had known, Apple would still have answered as he did, with a negative, for his chief hated to be unable to instruct.

"I am not surprised," Watkin said. "There are, of course, thousands of rallies, from the famous like the

Monte Carlo or the London-Brighton down to local affairs that don't even make the local papers. BOVA's is somewhere in the middle."

"Not exactly notorious," Apple helped.

Ignoring him, Angus Watkin went on, "Every spring the club organises a rally for its members, going from Paris to Vienna. It's a four-or-five-day thing, with points being awarded for this and that. The winner, not necessarily the first one home, receives a worthless cup. He also gets a measure of prestige, within BOVA circles, of course."

Apple nodded his comfortable understanding. "Of course."

"As you, Porter, are a member of the British Old Vehicles Association, I suggest you enter yourself and your car for this year's rally, which starts next week."

Apple glared the beginnings of panic. "But, sir. Look. I'm not. I'm not a member."

"Ah, but you are," Angus Watkin said, pleasure showing in the slight movement of one eyebrow. "You joined several months ago, your vehicle having been inspected and accepted by the BOVA committee chairman."

Apple lost his glare. Slowly nodding, he said in a small voice, "Which person has since died."

Lazily: "You could be right, Porter. All I know is that the gentleman in question seems to have signed these papers." He passed across an envelope. "They are in your real name. You will not need a cover."

Quietly crumpling the envelope as he tried to slip it longwise into his pocket, Apple asked, voice even smaller, "Is this a mission, sir?"

"It is, Porter."

Apple didn't mind when his nerve failed, when he

merely nodded instead of saying the desired, "Luckily, I'm available."

"The point of the mission you will learn in due course, Porter. Background will be supplied—time and place is given in the envelope."

Crisply, the pro: "Yes, sir."

"For the rest, prepare to leave and see to it that your vehicle is as close to its original state as possible, which includes colour."

Apple stiffened. "Colour, sir?"

"Colour, Porter," Angus Watkin said with another eyebrow shift. He began to get up. "Now if you'll excuse me."

The next minute Apple was alone, a tower of indecision but knowing that when he had finished balancing his yearning to be on a caper against having to dress Ethel in her widow's weeds of yesteryear, he would call Upstairs and tell them he was not available after all. An underling he may be, a flunky he was not. No Porter had ever been accused of lacking pride.

The woman said, "I do love to see these old taxicabs painted their traditional black."

"I know what you mean," Apple said.

"So often, sadly, one sees them made to look stupid with garish paint-jobs."

"That's terribly true."

Apple's responses were given absently. This was not because he was trying to pretend the exchange wasn't happening, that there had been no surrender to Angus Watkin. He had just realised that the woman, who had stopped beside him as he stood near Ethel on the pension frontage, had a familiar face. Her photograph, among several others, had been

shown to him the other day in a basement flat off
Baker Street.

Apple's mental wrestling over the widow's-weeds
matter had long been resolved. Surely, he had rea-
soned, Ethel, like all females, wanted to have her
finery changed once in a while. So to start with he
would give her that simple little black number they
all owned, changing it after a week or two for something new; something original and outrageous. He
would take her to the best firm in London. He would
spare no expense. He would, furthermore, make it an
annual event.

Thus had Apple created triumph out of chaos. Not
only did he have the caper, he had become a person
who was unusually understanding and generous, one
who could even be amused by Prunella Bank's saying, "People who tart up their old darlings ought to
be shot."

She was pretty. Her slim, big-eyed face and the
allure of long straight hair of a golden tone were
much more aggressive in the flesh than in a picture.
She was tall, her BOVA uniform was filled to a nice-
ness, her manner was friendly.

Apple introduced himself and clenched his toes
while establishing first-name terms. He said, "And
I'd like you to meet Ethel."

"Oh, she's yours," Prunella Bank said. "How nice.
My Agatha's a Buick. The 1938 Special."

"Much more graceful a series than the Super or the
Roadmaster," Apple said.

She turned to him with an eager smile, girl finds
boy more interesting. "You're so right, Apple."

Glad now of the coaching which had bored him in
that basement flat, Apple went on to share the talk of
prewar McLaughlin Buicks imported from Canada.

The lady, he mused, was totally unlike his expecta-
tions.

At twenty-seven, Prunella Bank, who had joined
BOVA three months ago, was owner-editor of an obscure quarterly. It published esoteric articles by unknown writers with unpronounceable names. All ref-
ugees from Eastern Europe, the writers had a single
theme: anticommunism. Copies of *White Truth* were
passed around openly in Iron Curtain countries,
where, Westerners claimed, it was thought to be a
humour magazine.

Delighted at having the reality be a lithesome creature with vampy eyes, not the stolid bluestocking
suggested by her background, Apple needed to remind himself that she was, all the same, one of the
Possibles. Therefore, he ought to keep emotionally
free.

Straightening from his intimate sag, in which one
arm dangled, Apple said a cold, "Quite." On the second of Prunella Bank's two slow, slow blinks he
sagged again with a warm, "I couldn't agree more,
Pru."

Their coziness, which had become personal (philology and *White Truth*, bachelor and spinster, Bloomsbury and Chelsea), was interrupted by two men. After introductions, they said they were making sure all
newcomers knew nobody dressed for dinner the first
night.

Apple was enthralled to see Prunella colour up
with an amateur pink. It made him feel blasé, skilled
and protective. He straightened; sagged.

Men leaving, Prunella asked, "What were we saying?"

The scream, long, seared around the parking area.
All talk began to fumble away like curtain-up while

every clank and engine-purr was stilled. Silence had reached purity by the time the screamer was winding down.

Apple had straightened again. He went farther, up onto his toes, in doing a fast scan of the area. Most people were also switching heads in seeking source; some, all in the same patch, looked to have found it, were staring toward a small blue sports convertible.

As Apple moved, so did everyone else. He had to push and hustle in making his way over to the blue car, not helped by having to tow Prunella, who was holding on to his sweater. They arrived.

The woman who stood with hand on throat staring at the hissing tyre, from which protruded an icepick, was close to sixty and near to fat. She had a skimpy covering of white hair, untidy as a defeated brush. Her face was a cram of features between bulges above and below, the brow of a genius, the jaw of a Mussolini.

The people who crowded around were telling each other to just look at that would you, in respect of the icepick, or telling the victim not to worry too much, some horrible foreign child must have done it.

A man walked her away with a soothing, "What you need, Mave, is a drink."

Mavis Whittington, a Possible, was an archaeologist. Since retiring recently from her post at a provincial university, she had joined every antique-car club in the country. A three-time widow, she lived in a Yorkshire cottage with two bulldogs and her blue MG. The determination evinced by Dr. Whittington's chin was proven by the fact that, on the kind of pension she received, she would have been wise to get rid of her dogs.

People were telling one another what they had

been doing when. "I was over on the other side, talking to Apple," Apple heard at his back, from Prunella, "when this blood-curdling yell came. Do you know Appleton Porter, by the way?"

He turned to be introduced to several people. While he was exchanging remarks about the incident he laughed inside, merrily, at the way his mind had suggested: She sticks an icepick in the tyre, darts away, finds someone to talk to as an alibi, mentions that as soon as possible after making sure she isn't left behind.

Excusing himself in case he was looking guilty about his thoughts, Apple moved away. Near the jabbering crowd's edge he met Enrico Balto, who told the sky:

"I was just on my way outdoors when I heard the Melba screech.

"I thought at least someone had been hurt," Apple said. "Wasn't it a bit overdone?"

The opera singer shook his long hair. "A trifle act three, yes, but comprehendible. Owners do get so attached to their vehicles that they can take these things as strongly as that. Or so I believe."

"Still. A piece of pointless vandalism by some child."

"Pointless?" Balto asked the back of a nearby Rolls-Royce. "Child?" He shook his hair again and walked on.

Turning from watching him go, Apple found himself facing a man of close to his own height. To his own surprise Apple said, "I was talking to someone over by my car when I heard the lady scream."

"I didn't ask you," the man said blandly.

"That's true."

"You're the only rally member I haven't met yet. I'm Jacob Planter."

Apple named himself while they shook hands. Next, he was again self-surprising, with, "You don't look too much like your photograph."

Frowning, the man asked, "Where did you happen to see a photograph of me?"

Since he couldn't very well say it had been in a flat off Baker Street, Apple waited for inspiration.

Jacob Planter, a minor inventor in the electronics field, was built like a pole-vaulter, hard with the height. About thirty, he had a dark complexion to go with the darkness of his eyes, his short hair, the Zapata moustache. Even his sweater was dark. He had the lordly stance and gaze of a customs officer.

As his likeness had never been in any periodical, Jacob Planter was beginning, when he tacked off into, "Ah yes. You must be on the committee. I sent in a photograph with my membership application, as requested."

Apple gave out a mumble before escaping thin ice by initiating the standard dialogue swapped by unusually tall people when they meet.

Although Planter's response was normal, Apple failed to collect the normal bonus of camaraderie. He reminded himself that inventors tended to be neurotic and that therefore he should sympathise, not blame, since it couldn't be much fun to be neurotic.

"Talking of which," Jacob Planter said, "I was watching the group here—from a distance. Someone told me what had happened and I didn't see any point in coming over, being like the other sheep."

"You're here now."

With Watkinesque deafness: "The only one I could

see clearly was yourself, you being a head taller than everyone else. And you know what?"

"No, I don't."

"You looked guilty."

"Is that right?"

"Quite amusing," Planter said. He didn't look amused.

Apple gave a soundless laugh, like taking a bite of air. "Yes indeed," he said. "I suppose I must have been putting myself in the place of the delinquent who did the deed."

"The odds in favour of it being the work of a nasty child are immensely long, Mr. Porter."

"Call me Apple, if you like," Apple said without enthusiasm.

"Sure," Planter said with less. "You old-hand rally fans always pretend these affairs're pure and decent. But everything I've ever heard, and just seen, says that they're as cutthroat as any other competitive sport."

Apple said, "Oh, come on. You don't mean you think one of the entrants stuck the knife in that tyre."

"Icepick."

"I didn't actually see it myself. I thought someone mentioned it was a knife."

Darkly, Jacob Planter said, "Icepick. That's what I was told. I had just come back from a stroll along the road there when I heard—"

"Please," Apple said. "You don't have to establish your movements to me, even though you do seem to know a lot about the affair. It's none of my business." He moved off smiling. "See you around, Jake."

Several times during dinner, with people sharing tables for six or eight and with the wine flowing, Apple forgot he was on a mission. It was the atmosphere, a what-next ticking of expectation.

Everyone acted bright and brimming, some bombardingly so, and there were even jokes passed around about that icepick. One version said the lady had done the job herself in order to get flirty with the pension's ancient porter, who had been given the task of damage repairing.

At one point Apple went to introduce himself to Mavis Whittington. She managed to be pleasant while weighing him up suspiciously and made him feel ten years old by calling him young Appleton.

As to the other Possibles: Jacob Planter was solemn, Adele Pringle happily chain-smoked throughout the meal, Enrico Balto politely declined to sing, Prunella Bank often caught Apple's eye from across the room.

The final Possible Apple met when the place beside Henry Caption was vacated, people beginning to drift out. Apple got up and went over, not so much with the caper in mind but out of worry that the next time his glance met Prunella's he might wink.

He exchanged names with the light-toned black man, who grinned like a small searchlight and said, "Sit down, friend. Have some wine."

Apple sat but held up a hand to the drink offer. "I want a clear head in the morning."

"Right you are. We start moving off at nine. It's a long way to Nancy."

"At least for our senior citizen cars it is."

"That's why we're skirting Switzerland," Henry Caption said. "Some of us would never make those climbs." He went on to tell of his 1935 Bentley, looking at his fingernails while dropping its Wakefield

slip-shaft, the Schmidt klaxon and a Darlington ran-
kle-pin.

Apple, impatiently waiting his turn, kept saying in
a dead tone, "Oh?" and, "Really?"

Born in Britain of a Jamaican mother and an English father, Henry Caption was a medium-built man
with a thick neck. His face always looked to be on the
verge of smiling, a twitch on the hover at his lips as if
he was waiting for the punch-line, but waiting without those clenches of worry, for, as his eyes told, he
knew he was bright enough to get it.

Twenty years ago Caption had reached transient
renown by breaking the world's record in the five-
thousand-metre race, this one week after a new time
had been set and a fortnight before the time was
shortened yet again. On retiring from competitive
athletics, the fourteen-days wonder became gym instructor in a private school.

Bentley finished with, Henry Caption went on
into, "So when my wife ran off with my worst enemy
this last winter, I decided to spread myself a bit."

"Ethel has—"

"I mean, what's the use of having a classic car if
you don't show her off?"

"Right," Apple said. "My Ethel—"

"I've got the thirty-*five*, don't forget, Apple. The
1936, as any fool knows, isn't in the same street."

"I didn't, as a matter of fact. However—"

"But that's enough about old cars," Henry Caption
said. "We fans can be such bores on the subject, right?
I wanted to tell you about a tyre-puncturing incident
before dinner."

Apple himself felt as though air was running out of
him. Settling, he said, "I know. Everyone knows.
Some rotten kid did it, they say."

"No, I don't mean the icepick deal. And if a kid did that one I'm Snow White with a wooden leg. Have you any idea how hard rubber is?"

"I hope you're not saying it was done out of spite by a BOVA member."

"No, that's what Jacob Planter said, and he said that you'd agreed with him. Myself, I agree with one or two who're saying it was done by somebody who wants to attract media attention."

"Well, that is possible," Apple allowed. "Somebody in need of the limelight."

Henry Caption gave his blazing grin. "Hey, that wouldn't be you, would it?"

While Apple, vaguely feeling famous again, was protesting too much that limelight was the last thing he wanted, he noted Adele Pringle leaving the dining room with Enrico Balto. He ended, "I don't think anyone here wants it."

"I wouldn't be too sure about that."

"But listen, Henry. What tyre-puncturing incident were you talking about?"

"On Prunella Bank's Buick, before the icepick thing. One of her tyres went down and she found a two-inch nail stuck in there. It could, yes, have been picked up on the parking lot here, if not on the highway."

"She didn't mention it."

"Or," Henry Caption said, "the nail could have been put in deliberately."

"More limelight?" Apple asked, looking around for the woman in question and finding she had gone.

"Or the fact that somebody doesn't like Prunella, for one reason or another."

Innocently: "Doesn't she run some kind of periodical?"

"Short stories or a deal like that," the ex-runner said, throwing the line away. "But back to you, Apple. Limelight was the last thing you wanted, you said. Is it liable to fall on you? I mean, are you in the news or something?"

When Apple had finished overexplaining that he had meant he was a retiring sort himself, plus telling about his job, Henry Caption asked, "Okay, so what brings a guy like you on a rally?"

Apple said, "Harmless fun."

That basement flat off Baker Street. It smelled damp. Also it was chill. Apple's feet had slowly become numb with cold over the hours, so that as he walked along the passage behind his informant, a wiry woman with the sunken eyes of insomnia or advanced television addiction, he clumped. Nevertheless, he was still able to view the situation not as meanly drab but as sordidly dramatic.

They stopped at a door. Over her shoulder the woman asked if there were any final questions, with a one-second pause before she knocked and said, "Good." On a call from inside to enter she pushed the door open. "Good-bye, One."

Perking at hearing again his mission number-name, Apple went in. He looked all around the dreary little parlour, noting lastly that the shadow in front of the window was Angus Watkin, who asked, "Is the ground prepared, Porter?"

"Everything under control, sir. Good evening."

"And your vehicle has been painted?"

That Ethel had been returned to black was known to Watkin, Apple knew, because he couldn't have missed seeing her in her parking slot right outside; he simply wanted to remind the underling of where the power lay.

Crisply Apple said, "An order is an order." By a slight shifting of the silhouette by the window he realised he had made an error. Smoothly he rectified by averting his eyes, a man crushed.

"Let's sit down, Porter."

When they were settled in chill armchairs in front of a hearth which held a crumple of red paper, when the woman had left again after bringing drinks, Angus Watkin said, "The subject is propaganda. The boosting and battering of national reputation, the saving and losing of face. The game we in the West play against Eastern Europe. You're with me?"

"Avidly, sir."

"What, in that game, Porter, scores the most points?"

Without hesitation Apple said, "When embassy people get expelled from the country for spying."

"No," Angus Watkin said. "That, in the general view, just makes the expeller look obtuse for having taken so long to find out about the spies."

Cunning, telling himself he was lying: "I never thought of that, sir."

"In reality, of course, the expeller has known all along about the spying but had no real need for an expulsion. When he does need one, it's usually for reasons unrelated to espionage."

"And anyway, the other side merely retaliates by kicking out a similar number of embassy personnel."

"True, Porter."

"Spies they've known about all along."

"False, Porter," Watkin said. "If they have the agents nicely under surveillance, contained, they'd rather keep them on than have to start over again with a new group."

"Certainly."

"So mostly they expell a few types who wouldn't know a cloak and dagger from a shawl and feather." He lifted his glass of whiskey. "Your health."

Obeyingly, Apple lifted his sherry on the rocks. But he lowered it again to suggest, "Defection?"

"Right, Porter. And we have been winning the game for years. Every Russian ballet dancer, every East German ice-skating duo, every coachload of Polish tourists who opts to stay on this side scores for Democracy. Ten points for your dancer and a five for the tourists."

"Whereas," Apple said, "the Reds have rarely scored more than a scruffy four. Some disgruntled housewife from Iowa or a rabid Marxist coalminer from Leeds."

As though there had been no interjection, Angus Watkin said, "There's a feeling abroad in the world, however, that things are going to change, that it's their turn to be on the winning side. Which brings us to what, Porter?"

"The BOVA rally," Apple said, though with hesitation, a quiz contestant hoping his guess would get lucky.

"Precisely. We have had a whisper relating to defection, when the rally ends, at a country hotel on the other side of Vienna. There are other whispers but this is the one which concerns Agent One."

"Thank you, sir."

"That hotel is close to the border with Czechoslovakia. It isn't easy to cross coming in this direction, covertly or otherwise, the populace having to be kept in. But there would be few problems in going over from here, especially if the person were expected and welcome."

"And one of BOVA's new members is planning to do that, sir?"

"So sayeth the whisper," Angus Watkin said. He drank.

"But the score won't be very high, sir," Apple said. "Nobody really famous is involved." He raised his glass but lowered it before lip-reach because Watkin had finished drinking. "I mean, we've got an opera singer of national repute, not international. A poetess known mainly on the literary scene. A small-time inventor. The publisher of an obscure magazine. A retired archaeologist. And an ex-runner whose name's familiar only in the world of athletics."

"That means little, the lack of fame," Angus Watkin said. "In each the other side could build up their prize into someone of great consequence. The defector isn't your housewife or miner. He has made a certain niche for himself. It can be turned inside out and stretched to a pillar."

"We can deny it."

"The louder we do, the more will it be believed that he is a person of consequence and value. Any one of those Possibles will score a nine."

Then why don't we just load the rally with agents in disguise? Apple had in mind to say. He stopped himself in time. Such a scheme would make Agent One either unnecessary or merely one among many.

In his disturbingly occult way Angus Watkin said, "By the by, Porter, the reason we don't cover the rally with our people is because the whisper could be totally false and is intended to keep us occupied while something is happening elsewhere. And something is."

"Why doesn't our defector simply buy a tourist ticket and fly to Moscow, sir?"

"That would be burning bridges. He might want to come back. It's not uncommon. A good percentage of those who defect to the West do go back again, but that doesn't hurt the score much due to the press tending to ignore returnees unless they happen to be big names."

"It's anticlimax," Apple explained. "Boring."

"If our defector does it this way he can always claim that crossing the border was a spur-of-the-moment thing, or he'd been abducted, or tricked, or he was drunk, or did it for a laugh, or crossed by mistake, and so on and so forth."

"Or he could say he did it to prove something or another."

"Whichever, you see the nub of the mission," Angus Watkin said, lifting his glass and drinking.

Apple raised his sherry, saying, "Yes, sir. To discover which of the Possibles is planning to defect and then try to change his mind." He put his glass down in time with Watkin, who said:

"I doubt if you'll succeed in doing that, Porter. It's his plans you'll have to interfere with, not his mind. One way or another, he has to be stopped from going across the border. It won't be all that easy."

"No, sir," Apple said with a touch of grimness, soldier about to climb out of the trench and charge.

"You might also have competition. There could be a KGB presence, someone giving the defector all the help he can, or even pressuring him to go through with it, a change of heart having taken place. The affair has, indeed, several intriguing possibilities."

One of them came to Apple now, abruptly and

painfully like a flick on the nose. It was not intriguing. Of himself Apple asked: What right have I to stop a person going where he wants?

Having no answer, he drank.

TWO

Apple couldn't help smiling when he came out into
the briskness and slanting sunshine. The air alone
was sweet enough to make him feel like a boy again,
as young as the day. Ambling among the cram of cars
and people, he gazed around vivaciously.

His eyes were full of the departure's bustle, his ears
of chatter and revs, his senses of a cavorting excitement, his mouth of the pastry-and-coffee breakfast
which had been brought to his room. The boy he felt
like was a voluptuary.

Already competitors were moving off, leaving every three minutes from a central position and in the
sequence that had been settled by last night's lottery
at dinner. The starter, one of the rally officials who
now all wore cap, dustcoat and neck-slung goggles,
an outfit circa 1910, had a way of glaring at a stopwatch and bringing down his go-arm as if victory
meant money, or defeat death.

Apple was moving on from watching ex-runner
Henry Caption zap off in a Bentley when he met
Adele Pringle. In a fine spray of ash from the ciga-
rette in her mouth she said, "Rod's okay."

"I'm sorry?"

"My car. Roderick. He's a 1929 Flying Standard.
And he hasn't been interfered with."

Apple shot away a worried look like a mum in a
playground, relaxing when the poet in yellow added,

"Neither has your taxi. It was just one of those things, yesterday's nonsense."

"I hope so."

"Or it was connected with the wagering."

Apple asked, "You mean the lottery?"

"No, the bets on performance some of the competitors make among themselves, to give spice. The odd one isn't above a little interference, I imagine."

"That's disgraceful."

"But the cars aren't rare antiques," Adele Pringle said. "Only old. Why, there's nothing before 1925. So it's naughtiness, not sacrilege." She moved on with an ashy cough plus a "Don't gamble."

I was thinking of the moral aspect, Apple didn't say, partly because it would have been ill-mannered, mainly because he had promised himself not to dwell on such matters for the time being. Almost, he could still taste the attack of sherry in his throat.

After discovering that a 1938 Buick Special was no longer present, Apple went to warm up Ethel.

By the time he drew alongside the starter, his number having been yelled around like an accusation, he had decided on sabotage as useful to his cause. Although he was declining to acknowledge that the idea had come from yesterday's punctures, he did allow that the catalyst was hearing about the wagers.

Apple reckoned that with a perpetrator being considered as either a nasty child, a limelight-seeker or a gambler out to nobble his rival, sabotage had sufficient explanations on hand to keep it from creating general panic.

A car that was disabled would serve two ways, as Apple saw the matter. If the owner was Defector, it could put him out of the rally, thus cancelling his plans, though he might elect to continue as someone's passenger; and if he did do that or grimly drove on, the fault repaired, it, his determination, would be strong evidence of him being the villain, so that he could be approached later.

And if the owner wasn't Defector, an innocent person who wanted to enjoy . . .

Apple interrupted himself with a strident whistle, which itself was cut off by a curt "Do you mind?"

The starter, arm raised like a quivering exclamation point, shot his eyes aside from their fix on his stopwatch. He said, tightly, "Trying to divert my attention is an old trick."

Aiming to make it up to himself for the innocent victim by dispensing a drop of kindness, Apple said, "You're an expert at the game, I can see."

Like a woman complimented, the arm swayed. Its owner murmured that he had, yes, done this once or twice before, to be sure, following which he hissed, "For luck, I'll give you fifteen seconds."

"Decent of you," Apple whispered, on account of it was the only thing to say. Next, spurting away from the arm-drop, he was musing smugly that it served him right, and let that be a lesson, all you needed to do was give a tainted whistle and you got involved in the spread of corruption.

Within minutes Apple was whistling again, cheerfully, as he and Ethel bowled along a peaceful country road, his elbow rakishly out of the window. He liked the competition from birds, the sun's tinge of warmth and the fact of him being Agent One at work.

A fork appeared. Pointing to the left was an arrow, a white cut-out on a stand a metre high. This meant that the right fork led to a main road, all of such which being avoided by the rally whenever possible, even though it meant covering a far greater distance.

As had been pointed out to Apple, it wasn't only a question of BOVA wanting the tranquility of the back roads and lanes; but that a highway's urgent traffic, particularly its commercial division, could get belligerent with the slow old cars which were pleasure-bent. Harassment was not unknown.

To consider that, remembering, Apple stopped whistling and driving. Both of these he started again, sending Ethel forward to the left, after missing fifteen one-second beats in his tune.

When Apple stopped the next time, an easy hour later, it was at a rustic café, though he needed to turn and go back to it since he had gone past before noting that one of the cars on its frontage was an old Buick.

After parking on the gravel, which had the friendly crunch of cereal, Apple argued back at a niggle that he was not, as he had suggested, here for social/romantic reasons, but caperwork. No one was above suspicion, not even the beautiful and charming Prunella Bank, who had the courage to do her own publishing thing.

Therefore, when he had wended through other cars to the wooden building, Apple, ignoring the entrance, stealthily and grumpily went to the window. In peering around its edge he cheered up, liking the spyness.

Among the French families with children sat Prunella. She was semi-facing this way at a table with a man. Apple, relishing the danger, had to crane far beyond the windowframe to get a good sighting on the man's profile and establish him as the inventor Jacob Planter.

He wore a smile. So did Prunella. They looked cozy together as Planter held out his cup for his companion to pour tea into it from a pot.

Yes, caperwork, Apple mused coldly, and that signified sabotage. At the same time Apple was agreeing that the Bank woman looked less attractive than yesterday and that in suspect Planter's smile there was definitely a hint of something rotten, to be conservative.

Humming in a hard key, Apple retreated and went back into the cars, where he sought out the reality of what he had seen in that place off Baker Street. Annoyingly, the car looked better than its photograph.

The 1936 Cord owned by Jacob Planter was a gleam of cream bodywork and chromium trim, with huge silver tubes coming out of the motor like a robot's expression of love. The canvas top was folded down.

Flashy, Apple sniffed as he brought out his penknife. With the gadget which tripled as toothpick, buttonhook and skeleton-key, he set to work on the hood's lock. That the engine covers of Buicks had no locks he managed to avoid bringing to the front of his mind.

Burglary done, Apple lifted the side-flap. Following another flash of annoyance (the motor's magnificence made Ethel's innards look like a sewing machine) he got busy on the carburetor.

While tinkering with his knife's screwdriver/canopener/nailpriser, Apple thought in part of that day years ago at Damian House when they had learned car disabling. From the most simple, blocking the exhaust pipe, they came to a variety of sophisticated methods, and the girl, the course's sole female, was always at the front when they were looking into

the motor and listening to the instructor. Her name
was Jean or Jane. The back of her neck had great
poignancy.

Apple had just finished and was putting his knife
away when he heard the footfalls. The crunch-
crunch, being made by one person, was coming this
way.

Apple's nerves jangled. He yanked down the flap,
heard the lock click half a second before he heard the
crunching splat louder, and flung himself backwards
while giving a yell of alarm. If caught in an awkward
situation, Training Five said, always create another
reason for your agitation.

Apple tripped. This wasn't part of the ploy. Not
that it mattered, though he wasn't fond of the gravel's
bite when he landed flat on his back.

The crunching stopped. The person standing
above him, feet by his head, was Prunella. His relief
countered by the glum fact that she wasn't wearing a
skirt for him to make an issue of not looking up,
openly, thus showing what a decent type he was, Apple said, "I nearly got stung by a wasp."

"Oh, you poor thing."

Apple allowed Prunella to help him upright, where
he held on to her hand until she started giving small
tugs, this after it had been settled that no damage had
been done and he had walked her well away from the
Cord.

For all-round smartness Apple awarded himself ten
out of ten. He felt sure he wasn't being influenced in
the scoring by his pleasure at Prunella's concern.

"How about a coffee, Pru?"

"No time," she said, wiping back her long hair at
both sides. "I don't care a fig about falling behind
schedule but I don't like to be too obvious about it."

"If you're not in the rally to win," Apple asked, smiling, "why are you in it?"

"To escape."

He twitched the smile. "Oh?"

"We all need that once in a while, don't we?"

Smile firm again: "Oh, I see. Escap*ism.*"

Prunella frowned, prettily, as though with practice. "I thought it was *es*capism. But you're the linguist."

"It's an act," Apple said. "Let's meet for lunch and I'll confess all."

"That sounds good so long as it's Dutch."

Minutes later, rendezvous chosen from a Michelin, Prunella had gone and Apple was crouching behind Ethel. That he couldn't see the Cord was unimportant; he could hear. His faint smile formed a cross between whimsical and cynical.

Jacob Planter came out, crunched to his car, got in. Next came the starter's whine. The motor coughed once, roared richly to life.

Planter drove away.

Slowly, slowly, Apple rose to the height he would have been if wishes were raindrops. His sag was due to mortification. He was sure he had done the right procedure on the carb but was pressured to admit that he possibly had lingered too long on that poignant nape.

Which meant it wasn't entirely Agent One's fault but partly Jean or Jane's, Apple allowed on going into the café. He ordered a pot of tea, with two teabags.

Break quickly over, Apple continued on his way. He had covered less than a mile when into sight came what made him sit tall with an imp's grin.

On the grass verge stood the Cord, its engine-flap up. Jacob Planter was stooped inside.

Apple composed himself in order to bowl sedately by. It was from the side of his vision that he saw the inventor, hearing an approach, straighten and turn, then stand there with his arms down and his head lowered and his face showing an expression of despondency.

What Jacob Planter looked like was your average sort of guy, a decent bloke, a hardworking man whose dream of a holiday had just fallen apart like a songbird shot out of the sky.

"No," Apple grated. But it was no good. The suggestion of ache in his chest lingered even though he had now passed the stalled car. With a sigh of defeat he stopped. He began to reverse.

"You don't *have* to stop," Jacob Planter called out, surly.

Walking toward him from Ethel, Apple said a freezing, "I'm aware of that."

"I mean, lots of other BOVA people've gone straight by."

"Did they wave?"

"Very funny. Riotous. Here I am, broken down on a deserted country road, miles from a telephone, and do I get help? No, I get wit."

Apple halted on, "Maybe you were being witty when you told Henry Caption I'd agreed with you that the icepick deal had been done by a BOVA member, out of spite."

"I don't recall saying that," Planter snapped. "And what's it got to do with me being broken down? Maybe you're trying to get out of giving a hand."

With his seethe under control, Apple stopped cursing himself for having given in to his all-heart impulse. He was glad. He would make such a thorough job of disabling the Cord that an expert would be necessary to put it back to rights.

"I stopped out of curiosity, not altruism," he said. "I owned a Cord once."

"Yes?" Jacob Planter said. "But you also claimed to be a Committee member, which, it seems, isn't true."

"I don't recall saying that. And why someone who's supposed to be an inventor can't fix a straightforward mechanism like this beats me."

With head tilted back Jacob Planter said, "That would be the same as asking a chef to make a sandwich. The simpler an object, the more foreign it is to me."

Muttering at a level that would be heard about device-snobbery and ball-racism, Apple went past and stooped into the engine. "Got a screwdriver?"

While fiddling with the carburetor Apple told himself he wouldn't think about Jane or Jean and the way the fine locks of hair swirled on her neck like flora in fairyland and that little fawn mole as appealing as an innocent forest creature which had got lost on its way home. He told himself this several times.

Straightening at last, satisfied, Apple said, "Sorry. It's more complex than I remembered. You'll have to get hold of a professional, in Paris."

Planter, sitting at the wheel, groaned. As though poking someone in the belly, he jabbed the starter. There was a whine—and the motor came to thrumming life.

While Apple glared in anguish, Jacob Planter, face bright, said, "That was more of your twisted wit, evidently." He raced the motor. "My, it's smooth. It's never run smoother."

Bitterly: "Thank you."

"I knew French petrol would be good for her, as soon as she got used to it."

Apple swung around with the precision of a clockwork soldier. He marched back to Ethel, got in, closed the door with supersoftness to give himself a lift by demonstrating his control, drove off with the gentle care of an old nun who was early for mass.

With as royal a disregard for logic as for person, Apple fumed: We go to the trouble of stopping, we lose precious time off the schedule, we repair his rotten flashy car—and we get absolutely no thanks. Not a word. Not a nod or a wink.

Apple was still drawing warm satisfaction out of feeling noble, and feeling abused on account of his nobility, and feeling proud for not having stopped to return the abuse, when he came to a crossroads.

The white arrow pointed right.

Apple was continuing to squeeze gritty pique out of knowing it would be dangerous to try nobbling the Cord again because Planter would suspect his hand, and knowing it was too late now to use the slicing, shattering jibe he had just thought of but should have tossed behind him as he left, when he brought Ethel to a stop and got out.

The road behind was clear. Mr. Planter would still be reassembling his immaculate pretty-pretty toolkit, no doubt, Apple mused viciously. He kept his mind off the fact that Ethel's toolkit was a thing of pristine beauty.

Apple picked up the arrow. He put it down again fast as from the other direction a car abruptly came. Until it had gone by he stood with hands clasped behind, lips pursed in the shape of a whistle, eyes aimed toward a cloud.

It was the work of thirty seconds to move the arrow several metres across the junction and turn it around so that it gave direction as being to the left.

Back in Ethel, Apple drove on. Inside him he had that gorgeous Xmas-morning sensation that comes from having been proven right or having scored a hit with your slipper on the yowly cat. Which, his grin fat, Apple saw not as being born of the vindictive but of pleasure in a smart caper move. Curtly he refused to face the question of what would be accomplished by causing Jacob Planter an extended delay.

A contiguous question Apple did, eventually, face, though with one shoulder raised in defence, was related to other rally competitors. Were they all, as he had assumed, ahead in the run, making Planter the last man, or were there still some behind?

The question didn't change from academic to reformatory, inquisitive to punitive, until Apple had driven for another hour. Both shoulders up against the idea of non-Possible BOVA members trailing off into the wilds, miles off their course and hours out of their schedule, he stopped where the lane widened as it passed through a hamlet.

Watched with interest by an old man who sat whittling in his doorway, Apple got out. He opened the engine to give the impression that he had a problem, explaining his halt. He bet himself two million pounds that if Jacob Planter had been on this road he would drive straight on by.

The only thing was, Apple didn't know what to do next. If there were other rallyers behind, they would follow the arrow into the wilderness. So did he have to go back to check?

Apple was forced to laugh at the absurd notion that he could possibly do anything so obtuse. That finished, he went to ask the old man, who might just have counted how many veteran cars had passed this way.

The man said, "What veteran cars?"

The rendezvous restaurant's parking lot was all but empty. Certainly it held nothing that resembled a Buick. Apple stopped there anyway and trudged inside, thinking in bitterness that he at least could ask the chef to make him a sandwich.

Only three tables had custom; the rest were being stripped by waiters who looked at Apple as you would at a thumb in your soup. One of them, however, handed him a note, with, "You have to be the tall Englishman I was told to watch for."

Prunella wrote that she had waited as long as she could, she hoped he hadn't had an accident, she had enjoyed a lovely lunch in company with Henry Caption, who was a real charmer.

As Apple jammed the note into his pocket he was waved at by a lone diner at a window table. It was Enrico Balto, Apple now saw. Going over he asked, "May I join you?"

The singer told the pepper-pot grandly, "You may, even though I am on the point of departure."

"I am somewhat cunctatious," Apple said, sitting. He wished people like Balto didn't bring out the pedantic worst in him. "See, it's because of the bloody arrow, like."

Watching the hairy singer with care Apple went on to tell what must have happened: someone had changed the position of the arrow deliberately so that it indicated the wrong way. He didn't go on to say that he had deliberately but unknowingly put it right thinking he was putting it wrong and then had taken the wrong way thinking it was right. He would only have got confused anyway.

"So you went wrong."

"Right."

Enrico Balto admitted to a tree outside, "Children are such a nuisance."

"It doesn't have to be kids. I had a competitor in mind."

With a flicked glance eye to eye: "Which one?"

Apple said he had meant any of the competitors. "Not one in particular."

A waiter came. Shaking his head in quiet triumph he said everything was off except the *saucisson aux lentilles* or *oeufs en meurette*. Apple said he would have them both. The waiter left with a sigh.

"It is so easy to dramatise these vicissitudes, Mr. Porter," the piratical tenor said melodiously to the napkin he was folding. "I myself am of the opinion that none of us gives a penny damn who wins the rally."

"Are you in it for fun?"

"I am in it for personal reasons. But you were going to tell me of the time you heard me at Covent Garden."

"Couldn't get tickets," Apple said.

Enrico Balto began to get up. "Must clean my teeth."

He still hadn't come back by the time the food arrived, both dishes together, but as Apple looked around more, relaxing and cheering with the meal, he saw him sitting at the bar with coffee and brandy. He had gone when Apple had finished his own coffee and was therefore making a mental note to ask another time about those personal reasons.

After paying his bill he strolled outside. All Ethel's tyres were flat.

Apple stood there in a droop of disbelief, election lost by one vote, wife elopes with midget. It just wasn't fair, as well as everything else.

Also there was Ethel herself. As any astute salesman knows, a flat makes the nicest automobile look unwanted at any price. With all four tyres down like hose around ankles Ethel looked as jaded as a woman of the evening when she greets the following dawn.

Furthermore I have just had an excellent poached eggs with a red wine sauce plus bacon and baby onions on croutons, Apple protested. The onpiling made all this seem worse, which made him feel better, took him away from the humdrumity of mere inconvenience toward the glamour of martyrdom.

Apple grew a wistful smile. It stayed in place even when, on looking closer, he discovered that the situation was not as sheer as he had thought. The air had not fled through a stab's wound but had been let out via the valves.

Apple took his smile inside, adding a touch more pain around the eyes. While asking if there happened to be a foot-pump he could borrow to remedy the assault of a rival, he managed not to tell about being misdirected into the wilds.

The manager was sympathetic. He supplied a pump, and as Apple worked kept sending waiters out to see how he was getting on. When all the waiters did was that, nodding encouragement and going in again, Apple lost the wistful bit.

In any case, he had no energy to spare for the operation of facial muscles. It was quite involuntary, that quivery and vacant sag of his features as he panted.

Never having before used a foot-pump, Apple was

finding the task something less than a joy. He felt as though he were running a marathon on one leg. Nor was there a lack of protest from poached eggs with a red wine sauce plus bacon and baby onions on croutons.

After each tyre was uppish, enough air in it to get him carefully to a service station, Apple lay like the dead on Ethel's back seat. As with the arrow-mover, on the air-releaser's identity he was keeping a closed mind.

Finally, some two hours after arriving at the restaurant, he was ready to leave. A waiter was there at once, causing Apple to not bother with expressions because he realised the attention had been to ensure the pump's nonremoval.

Following his creep to a highway service station for air, Apple put on speed to get back to the secondary road and to continue on his way. He yawned. He told himself dully that you couldn't say this was an uneventful caper.

At every arrow Apple laughed unsteadily and worried until he came to the next one, at which he laughed unsteadily and worried until . . .

Approaching yet another village, picturesque enough to be in movies, Apple, as usual, slowed. He had no intentions of getting stopped for speeding.

Ahead, midway along the straggly street, a policeman moved to the kerb. Apple slowed still more. The policeman, his gaze firm on Ethel, stepped into the gutter. Apple went even slower. The policeman moved out into the roadway. Almost at that area now, Apple reduced to walking speed. He was coming to a stop when the policeman raised a halt-commanding hand.

"It was no joke," Apple said.

They shook their heads in agreement, although two were still smiling, and Mavis Whittington suggested, "It was an adventure nonetheless, young Appleton."

"Have you ever been locked in a cell?"

"Don't recall that I have."

"Adventure's hardly the word," Apple said. He described the six-by-ten dungeon under the village police station without mentioning the true virulence, his claustrophobia. However, prickly tinges of it returned as he remembered standing on the bunk on tip-toe in order to see over the windowsill but having to sink down periodically into his fear: from bashing away at the foot-pump his thighs were as tender as bruises.

Henry Caption said, "And all because you'd run over a few chickens."

"That's what the police were told on the telephone. It wasn't true. I denied it but they arrested me."

"You poor thing," Prunella said. "That on top of your close shave with a wasp." She explained to the others.

Dr. Whittington mumbled, "Didn't know there were wasps around at this time of year."

Apple said raggedly, a strong whimper, "Well, it looked like one to me."

They were at a table in the bar of the hotel near Nancy. It was late, too late for dinner, when Apple had finally arrived in the deserted lobby. After checking in and washing, he had been eating sandwiches when Prunella, Caption and Dr. Whittington had entered, all in evening dress, all playing verbal variations of *We thought you were dead.* Only Prunella, it had seemed to Apple, looked genuinely pleased.

"They also thought it strange that I spoke unbroken French," he said. Now he wondered if perhaps his detention had been extended on account of him having corrected the sergeant's grammar. He had done it out of being aggravated with the way the desk official repeatedly looked down at the accused's lower legs as if he thought his height was some kind of gag.

"Anyway," Mavis Whittington said. "You were released."

"They finally came to the conclusion that it was a hoax, since the anonymous caller didn't call back or show up."

The three smiled again, unising, "Hoax?"

Apple said, "Maybe somebody wants me out of the rally."

They stopped smiling. "Ah."

"And before that, my arrest, there was the business of the misplaced arrow."

They all began to talk, not in unison but on the same theme: Adele Pringle had gone miles off course because of an arrow pointing the wrong way, although this was not generally accepted as true, to the poet's silent fury; the whisper was that she had said it to cover making poor time.

"We all thrashed the matter out at dinner," Henry Caption said, tweaking his bow-tie. "With two results. One, it's been agreed that we won't talk it up. We don't want to attract media attention."

"Two," Prunella said, "from here on an official will stand by every arrow till everybody's gone past."

"Fine," Apple said. "But did the out-thrashing come up with any answers to the who or why of the interference?"

Mavis Whittington: "Practical joker or idiot, child or casual passer-by."

"Nothing sinister?"

They shook their heads with slow uncertainty, like people impressed with the awful. Henry Caption said it was easy to make melodrama out of these things.

"That has a familiar ring to it," Apple said. "But I haven't told you about my flat tyres yet."

His audience was as avid as a desert for rain. Not until he had started on the story of how he had slaved over the second tyre, after giving every detail of his struggle with tyre one, did interest falter.

Henry Caption said he got the picture. "So if all this, from icepicks to arrows, is deliberate sabotage, not pranksters, idiots, passers-by or children, who is it being done by?"

"And," Dr. Whittington asked, "why?"

Prunella wiped both sides of her hair back. She said, "Even though I have possibly been a victim myself, and you, Mave, definitely have, I don't believe there's a serious plot afoot. I think it's being done out of envy."

Henry Caption asked, "On cars that're better than the guilty party's?"

"No, but that could be it. I meant the taggers-on and the groupies. Or locals who see us having a fun time."

An ecstatic time, Apple mused while saying, "I didn't know we had groupies."

"Oh, they're somebody's sister or cousin or whatever. That's where I place the blame."

"Personally," Mavis Whittington said, "I think it could be more than one person. Could be a dozen. I'm not saying it is, mind you. Just could be."

The ex-runner said, "You didn't bring this up at the discussion at dinner."

"It wouldn't have been polite."

Apple wondered what she meant by that. Henry Caption asked, "And the motive?"

"I don't know the emotion involved, other than animosity," the archaeologist said, sticking out her Mussolini chin. "Perhaps it's resentment. It doesn't show on the surface, I will admit. But we can't escape the awkward fact that, so far, it's only recent members who've been interfered with."

Caption said, "Oldtimers against newtimers."

Curious phraseology, Apple was thinking while Prunella said, "How horrid. I don't believe it for a moment. I think I'll go off to bed in a huff."

Dr. Whittington said, "We do have a clue, of course, in respect of young Appleton's anonymous caller."

The others said, "Yes?"

"Yes. He or she speaks French."

"I did think of that," Apple lied. "And as to sex, that wasn't mentioned." He smiled at Prunella.

"Another of-course," Henry Caption said, "is that the whole story could be a lie, and our tall friend here was late for some other reason." He smiled at Apple, who said:

"Thanks muchly. Decent of you. What reason could I have for lying and for missing a good dinner." He smiled at the stout archaeologist.

Caption said, "To take suspicion off yourself as the guilty party by saying you were nobbled." He smiled at Prunella, who looked at Apple with a headslant of reproach.

He said, "We could soon settle that by calling the police back there."

Caption: "Oh, I don't necessarily mean you weren't arrested. Since your French is perfect, you could have made that anonymous call yourself."

"You could, y'know," Prunella said with a hand movement that asked him to be fair. "You could also have moved the arrow and let down your tyres."

Mavis Whittington said, "And I could have ice-picked my own tyre and Adele Pringle could have moved her arrow, if it was moved at all." She smiled at Apple, who said:

"So maybe you, Henry, had better do something to your car or you might come under suspicion."

"Sure," the ex-runner said. He smiled to himself.

Prunella got up. "I really must go to bed."

The other two also rose. All saying good night and remarking that maybe this sabotage nonsense would be left behind tomorrow, when they crossed into Germany, they left the bar. Apple wondered if he ought to do Henry Caption a favour.

It was midnight. He had wanted to leave the job until even later but was so exhausted that it was painful to stay awake. Already, while standing rigidly with his back against a wall in his room in a Korean trick that was guaranteed to keep you awake, he had nearly dozed off, needing to snap his head up.

Rubbing the back of his neck, Apple softly left the room, softly went downstairs. Though brightly lit, the lobby was deserted. A television set was screening an American sit-com dubbed in French. From the ajar door to an office behind the reception desk came a murmur of voices.

Apple went over to the revolving door. Its swooshing took him outside, where he was brought to a halt by night's blackness, which is always deeper away from settlements. But the reason the rally was using country hotels, it had been explained to Apple often,

was their ability to accommodate several dozen vehicles.

Eyes grown partially used to the dark, at least so he
could see his way, Apple went on. Among the cars he
began to search for Henry Caption's Bentley.

He had stopped, was looking with wary interest
toward a car whose front was open, when he heard a
recently familiar sound. It was a swoosh.

Turning, Apple saw a figure come out of the hotel.
There was enough background light to show that the
person was either male or a woman with short hair.
After a pause the figure came into the cars.

Apple stood still, listening; it was too dark for him
to see more than a four-car distance. The footfalls
stayed at about the same pitch, but then took on an
erratic pattern as though their maker was wandering
around in one spot.

Apple started to go in that direction, taking his
time, a wader's creep. Because of his tender thighs he
went flat of foot rather than tip-toe. As he drew
closer the footfalls were joined by metallic clanks,
hums of concentration, grunts of effort.

The area all these sounds were coming from, Apple
saw at last, was beside the car he had been looking
for, and that they were being made by its owner he
established following his final metre of creep.

Looking through the windows of two intervening
vehicles he saw the ex-runner, who was busily at
work. He appeared to be operating a jack.

Apple kept an intrigued watch for fifteen minutes,
at the end of which Henry Caption stooped away,
rolling the wheel he had removed from his car. He
went out of hearing beyond the parking area; returned within minutes, wheelless; went back into the
hotel.

With a flashlight from Ethel, Apple soon found where the wheel had been hidden in tall weeds. It took him five minutes to put it back on the Bentley and let down the jack, which, with other tools, he left neatly on the running-board.

If Henry Caption was going to be nobbled, Apple mused, moving his shoulders as though they prickled, it would be by Agent One, and thoroughly, not by said Mr. Caption, who was trying to take suspicion off himself.

That personal considerations were getting in the way of caper thinking, Apple held in a mental shed, turning a deaf ear to the thuds.

He went to the car whose engine-flap was lifted. He recognised Adele Pringle's Standard. With his flash he looked in at the motor, finding vandalism, superficial but thorough: all leads had been disconnected, from battery, spark plugs, distributor, and everything that could be uncoupled had been pulled asunder.

When Apple started to put the motor back to working order it was because, A, with this on top of the misplaced arrow people would think Adele was protesting her non-guilt too much; B, if she hadn't done it herself, it was a rotten trick; C, he wasn't about to add to the damage and render the car useless as per his overall plan on account of, well, how could a poet possibly be a turncoat?

Apple, blinking tiredly, was still tinkering when he heard that woosh again. He doused the light fast, rose to look over at the hotel entrance.

The person who had come out was either a woman or a man with long hair. S/he, armed with a flashlight, went quickly to one of the cars. Next came a hiss. When it continued unbroken Apple stopped thinking the person was looking for cats or aiming to get someone's attention. He knew what it was.

This he firmed by going over there at his wade. That he was able to resist shouting, "What're you doing there?" he considered pretty solid of him.

On arriving near the car, a 1948 Austin, Apple wasn't particularly surprised to see that the one kneeling by a front tyre to let out its air was Enrico Balto, the car's owner.

Again Apple was able to resist impulse, this time to saunter over and say, "You've obviously had a lot of experience at doing this, especially today."

Instead, when the hissing stopped, he gave a harsh laugh. He did so with his head turned away to confuse source.

The opera singer shot to his feet. The flashlight he zoomed all around without hitting the place where Apple crouched. Light down, he hurried back into the hotel.

That was Apple's last moment of cheer. Finished putting Adele Pringle's motor back in order, he went into the hotel lobby, where, with a dirge in his heart, he asked to borrow a foot-pump.

THREE

The rally members who stopped Apple downstairs next morning did so with offers of sympathy for his travail of yesterday, and eagerly, as if what they factually wanted was to let him know they were aware of what had happened, were in possession of every mouthful of rally gossip.

They tapped his bicep, said too bad, mentioned where they were at about the time his tyres were let down, frowned hard to show they weren't amused, not in the least, about that anonymous telephone call that landed him in a cell and said the whole incident just went to show the dangers in learning foreign languages.

Apple smiled complacently at everything. He was rested and bright. The attention he enjoyed. Being reminded of his dungeon experience made him feel pleasantly jaded. He dawdled by a final group of ralliers in order to give them the chance to make their offers of sympathy.

When they merely nodded he didn't mind. And when Adele Pringle drew alongside him as they were both on their way out he laughed at her, "Good morrow, chicken killer."

"Good morning, Miss Arrowed." He thought that quite nifty and reminded himself to tell someone he had said it.

"You had a portion of that too, I understand."

"But I didn't kill any chickens."

"Oh, come on. We've all blasted a hen or two in our day. What motorist hasn't?"

"I haven't," Apple said. Feeling unjaded and a prig he added, "I suppose if I did, I'd stop."

Around her cigarette Adele Pringle wheezed a smokey "More fool you."

In a low voice Apple said, "I'm only kidding."

He had stopped despising himself, plastering that over with admiration at his inventiveness in keeping a conversation going, by the time he arrived with the poet by her car. At its normal state she appeared unaffected. Apple left.

He missed seeing Henry Caption's reaction to his wheel's presence by being intercepted by an official, who told him his position number from last night's lottery; but he was hovering within sight of the Austin when its owner approached.

Enrico Balto slowed. To get a better sighting on the front wheel he began to move his head about like a Balinese dancer. His eyes grew an expression of fret. They shot back to the wheel after every checking glance elsewhere—the car itself, the other tyres. Closing in warily he squatted for a good fret at close range.

Apple went over. "Problems?"

In looking up sharply, the singer overbalanced. He plopped onto his bottom and for a moment his heels dithered against the ground like a feeble display of temper. At space he snarled, "Must you steal up on people that way?"

Apple offered a hand. "Sorry," he said, in thorny truth. He would much rather see people lose their minds than their dignity.

Ignoring the hand Enrico Balto got up. He made

swipes at the back of his jeans. "You wanted something?"

"I wondered if you'd heard what happened to me yesterday."

"Only about ten times," Balto told his Austin. "Anybody would imagine you had suffered an extended series of enormous catastrophes."

"Seemed that way to me."

"Saw an arrow incorrectly through inattention? Got caught for killing chickens? No one to blame but yourself."

Apple said, "There was also the trifling matter of all my tyres being let down. Oddly, it happened at the restaurant where we met."

"If you were a more worldly person, Mr. Porter," the tenor said to his ignition key, "you would know that many café stops have arrangements with garages. One does the damage, the other repairs it."

Stiffly: "I don't believe that."

"Excuse me. My number's getting close."

It wasn't until Apple was driving, steering along a lane in sunshine, that his grumpiness changed. Feeling able to admit that Enrico Balto could be right, he became even grumpier.

From pointing out that in his own case it wasn't likely the manager would have loaned him a pump if there had been a café-garage conspiracy, no softening came, fortunately. Apple didn't at all mind the occasional bout of grumpiness. It made a nice change from his norm of contentment, which he wouldn't have cared to have people know about.

The morning passed without event. Every junction where a switch of direction needed to be indicated, the arrow was accompanied by an official in 1910 outfit.

Apple's spirits were back to disillusioning normal as he came to the German border, behind other ralliers. They were all waved through by Customs and Immigration men who wore the kind of tight smiles adults wear at school plays, except during their own kin's appearances, when the smiles get floppy.

Apple drove on in countryside no different from before except for the design of buildings and a certain overtidiness, a suggestion that the grass had been brushed and the trees combed.

After turning at an official-guarded arrow, getting off the main highway again, Apple began to see rally people having picnics. That made him burp with hunger. He told his stomach they would stop at the next eating establishment, whatever its type, though the more expensive the better, since their host was Upstairs.

When Apple did stop, however, minutes later, it was because he had seen, drawn off the road with two other rally cars, a familiar Austin.

He parked around the bend, in a farm gateway, liking the idea that a vehicle might roll up there at any moment; liking the risk. He walked back with Ethel's toolkit.

First Apple established the whereabouts of the three cars' occupants. This he did by following the sound of singing. It led him in a cautious prowl through trees to where he could see, beyond the copse, Enrico Balto, arms spread, serenading three rapt matrons—two drivers and a co-pilot. The tenor was standing by, his audience sitting on, the Persian rug whose centre held a lavish lunch, complete with champagne in a bucket.

His resolve hardened by the sight of a ham-and-veal pie which he would never know, Apple returned to the cars. He didn't dawdle. Any of the picnickers could appear, now that the singing had ended, as well as there being the danger of that blocked gateway.

It was a simple matter to remove the carburetor.

Now Enrico Balto was out of the rally, Apple mused as he walked away. Getting a replacement for a model that old would, if possible at all, be a project of several weeks' duration. The only suspicion Balto had to worry about from here on was in respect of his intentions beyond Vienna—if he continued in the rally as a noncompetitor.

Who, Apple reminded himself, might be totally innocent, even though pompous, egocentric, immodest and unpleasant, as well as a feaster on ham-and-veal pie.

Apple queried what he was going to do with the carburetor, which somehow, eerily, felt like an artificial heart. He could bury it or hide it in Ethel somewhere. The latter could mean trouble. What if she was secretly searched, or if it was suggested that everyone submit to a search voluntarily? The danger would be constant.

Being firm with himself, Apple opted for burial. Using a screwdriver he cut out and lifted a sod, made a hole and put the carburetor to rest. Sod back in place, he cleaned the tool thoroughly before returning to Ethel, when he saw the note on her windshield.

The minor lane was off the rally route. Apple, driving slowly, kept a lookout for landmarks and, one at a time, waved his arms in the air. Before leaving he had dipped a rag in Ethel's fuel tank in order to clean the grease off his hands, which now had to be cleared of the petrol stink.

So as to stop dwelling on the probability that he was heading into some kind of trouble, an ambush, a wild-goose chase, whatever, though he had to follow through regardless, Apple was acknowledging that Ethel might have been noted within range of the Austin by other ralliers, which could come out when the sabotage news hit. He ought to create a cover story.

Acknowledgement over, Apple went back to his dwell. It seemed certain that only villainy could be behind *Join me for a picnic lunch, if you like. PTO and X marks the spot. Yours, P.*

The penciled words were in block capitals, the map on the other side was skillfully drawn and had an in-scale appearance, Apple offered in evidence. Would Prunella Bank write like that, if, indeed, she had written this at all? Could she have made the map, since women, traditionally, were hopeless about directions? How would she know this area well enough to plan an off-route picnic, unless . . . ?

Not knowing what he meant by that, Apple waved both arms vigorously. After grabbing the steering wheel in time, tree missed, he became stern from the thought that someone might be watching; and when he smelled his hands, stink gone, he pretended for the possible someone's sake that he was scratching his top lip.

By a building indicated on the map Apple made a turn. Over a rise he came within sight of a 1938 Buick Special, which reduced jeopardy's potential. He stopped behind the Buick on the wide verge and got out with near caution. Nothing happened.

"Coo-ee!"

Apple swung around. Waving at him from beyond a low wall was Prunella. "Come on," she called. "Everything's ready."

Over the wall, cautionless, even swaggering slightly because of having been invited here as a solo by the beauteous Prunella Bank, publisher, Apple went to where the scene looked ready to film one of those happy-family TV commercials forged by bachelor directors: tablecloth and napkins in red-and-white checks, cushions, patterned crockery, plates of goodies, kettle steaming on a fire; these set against neat grass, trees and a nearby stream.

Apple enthused while Prunella explained about the holiday she had spent at Freiburg two years ago. "Staying with a friend."

"Romance will out," Apple said, forgivingly.

"She's female, as a matter of fact."

"Nothing like a wonderful foreign holiday."

"I was bored stiff," Prunella said, lowering herself to a cushion. "So I rented a bike and spent the last week exploring the countryside."

"Light dawns."

"And I knew that one sunny day I'd return to this treasure, bringing someone nice to share in the pleasure."

Apple blinked, moved. He said, "That's poetic."

Prunella smiled inside her hair. "Do sit down."

With the delicate sandwiches, tarts savoury and sweet, pies of plum and of rhubarb, biscuits plain or chocolate, all lapped up with hot tea, Apple talked intermittently of West German politics and Staffordshire crockery; Prunella of her indecipherable handwriting and the hours she had spent as a child drawing pirate maps with her brother.

While, meal at a pause, they strolled along beside the stream, Apple talked about autobahns and the man who had invented road surfacing, John McAdam; Prunella about flowers and trees, birds and bees. Their bodies bumped once or twice so to prevent a reoccurrence Apple stayed at a reasonable distance.

On the return walk they stopped by a weeping willow. Its trunk had the willow's slope of grace: graceful in its inclination, gracious in allowing its branches to cascade toward the water.

This Prunella mentioned as she leaned her back on the trunk. Increasing still more the effect of her slope away from Apple, she put her arms above her head, which increased also the perk of her breasts.

She said it was terribly romantic here. Apple, after clearing his throat, said it was a pity they didn't have some music to complete the picture.

"It's not important," Prunella said.

"Or Enrico Balto to sing."

"I like it the way it is."

Irked at hearing himself mention the tenor, about whom he wasn't feeling the least bit guilty, Apple went on, "What I wanted to say was, or Jacob Planter to invent a musical instrument."

Prunella eased her head off the wood. In a drone she said, "Or Adele Pringle to quote a poem."

"Right."

"Or Henry Caption to run in circles."

"Well . . ."

"Or Dr. Whittington to dig a hole."

"Oh, I don't think so."

"Or," Prunella said, drone gone, "you and I to dance."

She came languidly off the tree and into his arms and he didn't have time to observe that dancing without music was difficult enough in itself, never mind the fact that they were on grass, before he realised that he and Prunella were kissing.

The kiss was romantic. More sensuous was the way their bodies, pressed close, weaved and swayed like linked stalks in a breeze, although with one part of his mind Apple was allowing that you could hardly call it dancing. Most parts of his mind were concerned with activities only vaguely related to the dance.

Prunella drew back, smiling secretly, as people will when they have lost a secret. She said, tone congratulatory, "That was bold of you, Apple."

"I'm quite a rogue, aren't I?"

"Come along." She took his hand in moving away. "We have a picnic to finish and a schedule to sort of keep."

Back on cushions, chatting, they had more biscuits and a slice of seed cake. Apple accepted a cup of tea even though he knew it would be bitter by now. When this proved to be so, no miracle having happened, he drank most of it rather than do a surreptitious emptying.

The yawn that engulfed him felt wonderful. "Think I'll take five," he said. He lay down beside the tablecloth and fell asleep at once.

Apple woke up slowly. That he began to awaken at all was because he felt chilled. The blankets had gone astray and he kept groping for them to cover his nakedness. The process of coming out of sleep started to quicken when not only did his hand fail to find the covers but everywhere met what was most unusual on a bed—grass.

Apple opened his eyes. He was out in the open, not in a hotel room. He had no bed, no blankets. The only thing true was that he had no clothes on.

Following Training Four's advice, Apple lay still

until by wriggles and flexings he had tested every
section of his body for damage. He found none. He
did discover that present was his wristwatch, from
which he learned that he had been out for around
two hours.

Shivering in spates he sat up and looked all around
at the desertion. He remembered everything from before, up to his sleep, which might have been caused
by something in the tea—that bitterness. The drug
could have been slipped into the pot while they were
strolling by the stream.

Which, Apple mused, could rule Prunella out as
perpetrator. Though she might be a cohort, or a victim herself, or have nothing whatever to do with it.

Of the picnic there was no trace, not even a disappointed ant. One of the napkins would have helped,
Apple thought in respect of his nakedness, the sense
of which he didn't get. As a prank it was anile, as a
warning of some nature it was weak.

Apple got up. With his spread hands hovering in
the region of his crotch he went toward the wall. In
his luggage in Ethel there were plenty of warm
clothes.

Long before reaching the wall Apple stopped. He
stared at the emptiness.

No Ethel. She wasn't there. Ethel had gone. She
had been taken away. There was no Ethel.

Staring on at the empty lane, Apple continued repeating to himself the fact of Ethel's absence, making
it believable, as he had difficulty picturing another
person at the wheel and therefore was troubled by
the odd notion that Ethel had gone off by herself.

He believed. So there were no clothes available,
warm or otherwise. And he needed some kind of

cover to see him back to the rally route, where he could get help from other competitors.

Scouting about for something to use, a large leaf, a discarded newspaper, Apple found nothing. He gave up, stood there shivering.

Pneumonia would certainly put him out of action, Apple agreed, if that was the perpetrator's plan. Warmth was needed fast. But there was nothing to start a fire with and he had scored a zero in those survival courses.

Telling himself the old chestnut about making a fire by rubbing two boy scouts together didn't give Apple a smile, the corn of it made him blush.

With that, he perked. Light though the blush was, it had caused him to feel five degrees warmer.

He got ideas.

When the heat faded Apple tried to remember another corny joke. He couldn't, which didn't surprise him, since jokes were among his pet dislikes.

After thinking that same chestnut again and getting nothing, even though he pretended he hadn't heard it before, Apple tried a different but obvious tack. He imagined himself walking into the United Kingdom Philological Institute, nude like this.

The resulting blush warmed him up, stronger than before, and he prolonged it beyond the normal by giving his imagined self first a tie, next a hat, last a pair of socks, which he made orange to begin with but then changed to blue because he didn't much care for orange.

While this was going on Apple had returned to considerations of cover. He saw where he could construct a rough kilt from willow fronds. With chill's return he went over to the stream and began breaking off branch ends, not without a wince for the destruction of both life and elegance.

During the rest of his couturier work, stringing fronds together on another of a fine suppleness to serve as girdle, Apple held off shivers with a front-row seat in the theatre of his imagination. After each production the programme changed, for repeats were found to have minimal effect.

He watched himself, still naked, take his dog for an outing in the village near to where Monico lodged; stand at a bus-stop in Piccadilly Circus; stroll into his favourite Bloomsbury pub; ride a bicycle along Charing Cross Road.

With the girdle in place, its ends held together in one hand, Apple had a hairy green kilt that reached his shins and hid efficiently that which civilization calls shameful. He set off along the lane, his bare feet wary.

Soon Apple found that, like repeats, picturing himself naked was losing its power. Shivering, he sought, and found, a substitute. He settled cozily in his front-row seat.

Apple saw himself, fully dressed, running along the village street after Monico, who was being chased by a cat; pushing, at a bus-stop, past other people in the queue to get aboard first; strolling into his favourite pub and ignoring completely the barmaid's pleasant "Evenin', Mr. Porter"; riding a bicycle along Charing Cross Road, on the sidewalk.

The blushes created by these and others similar, unawarely to Apple, were far stronger than those from the naked scenes. What he did, acutely, have awareness of was the incredible fact that his blushing was serving a purpose not only useful but invaluable. Never in his most untamed dreams had he thought the day would come when he would be glad of, even grateful for, his tender affliction.

He was past the landmark building before starting to accept that, by now, the ralliers would surely have gone by, although there still could be one or two stragglers. The poor speed he was making was due to a combination of being barefoot and having to carefully hold his kilt in place.

But as there was no one around, Apple realised, he didn't actually need the kilt at this stage. He stopped. After getting back to warm by watching himself saunter out of a bookstore without paying for the novel he had picked up, Apple removed his sylvan creation and rolled it neatly.

He set off at a loping run. Landing on the balls of his feet to reduce contact with the ground, he was able to make fair time. Apart from the bounciness of things he had no discomfort. He would have accompanied himself with a song if he could have thought of something appropriate.

Out of his theatre seat—the lope was keeping him warm—Apple gave his mind to what he had been avoiding: Ethel. At once he decided she would come to no harm, that the perpetrator had to be connected with the rally and therefore, whatever else he might plan, would have respect for a distinguished older vehicle.

So Apple knew there was no sense in imagining Ethel lying broken in a ditch, or being attacked by brutes with sledgehammers, or having her back hacked off so that, as a truck, she could be used in the gross, lower reaches of the transport world, wherein she would labour night and day with foul-mouthed shift-drivers until she collapsed, when, receiving no attention, she would be bundled into some bleak corner and left to rot.

Apple started to sing. His voice was unsteady and the song had no connexion with what was happening mentally or physically, but he gave all his concentration to the act and felt better.

And didn't notice the three women at first. Alerted by the singing, they straightened from their furrow-stoop and looked over the wall. They watched the approach with placid interest.

Apple noticed. His first cerebral move was to recognise, through clothing, colouring and feature, that the women were Turkish immigrants. His second move was to remember he had no clothes on.

With a gasped end to his singing Apple tried, all at the same time, to stop, to turn away, to centre his rolled kilt as cover, to signal with a smile and a gesture that there was nothing to worry about.

The result was a strange twirly grinning jig. The kilt fell. Crouching down to it with legs closed Apple called out in Turkish that he was a harmless sun-worshipper.

The three women exploded into noise and action. Raging that it was pigs like him that gave his compatriots in this country a reputation for outlandish behaviour, they began to throw missiles.

Apple protested that he was not a Turk. He did so to each woman in turn while offering silly-misunderstanding nods, while from his squat dodging clods and pebbles, while trying to unravel his kilt. It started to come apart.

"Pig!" the women ranted. "Beast!" Their aim was improving.

As a second clod of earth scored a direct hit Apple voted for discretion. Grabbing up the bundle of fronds he loped off, twisting sideways as he drew level with the women, one of whom began to climb over the wall.

Then Apple was past and a pebble clonked on the back of his head. He ran faster. He hissed at the lane's attack on the balls of his feet, grunted at the bounce, cried out whenever a missile struck.

A glance behind showed that the chaser, younger than the others and with a flourishing moustache, was making excellent time. With nothing left to throw she limited herself to insults, all of which related to sex. He was a rapist, an exhibitionist, a despoiler of defenceless women, a pervert.

Apple ran faster. On his next glance back he saw that the other two women were out of sight and that the third had not fallen behind.

With a plaintive edge in her voice she called out that she knew his terrible type. Insatiable. Just wait till she got her hands on him, swine that he was. She would show him. If she could. She was pretty defenceless herself, now that her husband had gone home, on account of that cough. And her friends were far behind so wouldn't hear her cries for help, if, indeed, she had the strength to make any after all this running.

Apple went faster yet. The woman's voice grew fainter. It trailed off into silence, her accusation that he had made her so tired she was going to throw herself down in a field and . . .

Apple went around a bend. A look back showed him he had finally lost the chaser. Despite that and the attack on his feet he kept up his speed. Taking the next bend brought him to the rally route.

It was devoid of traffic. Hastily Apple dropped his bundle and knelt to get it into order. Lungs heaving, nerves rattled, he dithered with the fronds and did more harm than good.

On hearing a car's approach Apple debated, briefly, whether to hide or make the best of it. Hiding wouldn't get him anywhere. With the bundle held before him he got up. He looked perfectly respectable, he assured himself.

The car appeared. Part of the rally, it was being driven by a retired bank manager and co-piloted by his sister, who was already pointing an unsure finger.

Sleepy-eyed with relief, Apple used both hands to hold the fragile bundle in place to be doubly safe, the while communicating his need of assistance by making that kind of face, by rocking his shoulders and by jerking his head backwards.

He was feeling slightly dizzy when the car drew level. Still communicating, it was in darts and flashes that he saw how thoroughly he was being ignored. The man had his eyes firmly on the road, as poor drivers do, the woman, her chin up, was making an observable issue out of staring in the other direction.

Like a mechanical toy switched off, Apple sagged immobile, except for the meagre movement of his head as he watched the car go on its way. He swung back fast on hearing another vehicle and switched on again.

The coming car wasn't old but that it was part of the rally, that, in anxious fact, it was the ultimate auto in same, showed by the driver's cap and the stack of arrows in the back.

Sinking himself into a semi-sitting position, Apple gripped the bundle between his thighs so that it stuck hidingly upright. Both arms thus free, he began to wave. Also he put on his assistance-needed face.

The rally official, a small dour man with whom

Apple had exchanged nods, the kind of man destined to pick up leavings, narrowed his eyes as he neared, scrutinising Apple's body and angled legs and the bundle. Despite manic waves, he failed to raise his scrutiny to the waver's face. Then, with a perplexed shake of his head, as though he couldn't figure out what product was being promoted, he had gone by.

With another car coming immediately, Apple had no time to despond. He would accept help from anyone. Making the angle of his crouch more acute as the bundle slipped out of perpendicular, he went on with his waving.

The car slowed. In it was a uniformed policeman.

The room was hospital-neat and had the smell of a gargle. There were no flies. The middle-aged officer behind his counter looked as if he had just come back from full treatment at the barber's, shaven to a redness, clipped to within an inch of his head. He almost steamed.

The traffic policeman finishing his say, he asked, "What about the evidence?"

"The evidence?"

"The collection of twigs. The birch."

"We left it, sir."

"It was only to cover myself with," Apple said. He wore a brown leather overcoat. It was several sizes too small. That had no importance in respect of length, since the hem reached halfway down his thighs, and the policeman had managed to get the buttons fastened; but Apple was clenched so tightly in the armpits that he couldn't lower his wrist-naked arms to his sides or move them much any other way from their out-poked position. In defence against a suspicion that he looked farcical, he was ignoring his state of dress and maintaining a bright mood.

The officer asked, "You left the course of a rally you're on, you found an isolated spot, you undressed to sunbathe, you dozed off, you awoke to discover clothes and car gone?"

"That's it in a nutshell."

"And you insist you're British?"

"I do. But I can worsen my German, if you like."

"It could all be true, of course," the officer said.

"What reason would I have for running around the countryside stark naked, risking my death of cold?"

"There are lots of obscure and obscene reasons. We get all kinds through here. You'd be surprised."

"And why should I say I'm British if I'm not?"

"It's true there was a rally," the policeman told the officer as though in apology, eyes round. He was full of his superior's importance.

Apple said, "I'd appreciate it if you people could get out a call on my car."

"That will be done," the officer said. "First, let's have a couple of answers. You have no identification to show, after all. You could be anyone. So, what's your destination?"

"I was told the hotel's name and the nearest town this morning but I've forgotten," Apple said. "No problem. I was going to follow the others."

"I see. Good excuse. Neat."

"Look. This can be very easily resolved. One of the rally officials went by right before the patrol car. You can call ahead, have him stopped, bring him back here. He'll be able to identify me."

"We could try that, yes, before we proceed."

Waiting on a bench, knees primly together and fingertips managing to touch the wood, Apple didn't mind the delay, didn't care that his feet were cold and sore, and didn't worry about having committed a caper no-no: involvement with the police. He was starting to get seriously concerned over Ethel. All this, after all, could be the work of a plain ordinary thief. With forged papers Ethel could disappear into the back streets of Berlin or Munich and never be seen by her owner again.

Apple fretted and fumed.

At last the traffic policeman came in, followed by the rally official, who looked as happy as a beggar on duty. He had a straggle of chin hairs that was trying to be a goatee. It quivered.

After a disinterested glance at Apple the official said loudly, "I demand an explanation. I demand to see the British consul. This is outrageous."

The older officer, appearing behind his counter, asked Apple for a translation. Going over there Apple said, "He wants to know why I'm being held." His mood became bright again.

"You're not being held. You're being assisted."

The rally official said tautly, "What is all this about and who, if I may ask, are you?"

"My name's Appleton Porter and I'm in the rally, a member of BOVA. We've met, you and I."

"I never saw you before in my life."

"I don't always dress like this."

Officer: "What's he say, what's he say?"

Apple told him, "He's never heard of anything like this before in his life."

Leaning forward, pointing at Apple while addressing the rally official, the officer asked, "Britischk?"

Hotly the little man said, "Who knows? There's so many of 'em around now, the young English hooligans. It was all right when they stayed at home and destroyed football matches, now they're travelling abroad and giving the mother country a bad name. Should be shot, the lot of 'em."

Apple translated, "Yes, British to the backbone. A truly fine man. If only there were more like him to go abroad and let people see what the British are really like."

Doing his pointing again the officer asked, "Ralleee?"

"Is he in our rally?" the little man said, aghast. "I should say not. There is a chap named Porter, I think, but he seems a decent type and nowhere near as tall as this fella."

Apple translated, "Why, he's a member in extremely good standing. He's a grand chap, is Porter. I think he's the most decent type we have. Stout fella."

Officer to Apple: "He doesn't sound happy about it."

"He's annoyed that anyone would doubt my bona fides."

"Is he willing, then, to vouch for you?"

Apple asked the rally official, "Do you absolutely deny that I am a member of BOVA?"

Nodding with emphasis: "I do, I do."

"There you are."

The officer asked, "And therefore willing to take you on to your hotel?"

"I'm afraid he can't do that. Against the rally rules. We aren't even supposed to speak to one another."

"So what're we going to do about you?"

Apple stopped feeling bright. If he wasn't careful, he saw, he was going to be stuck here, without clothes, car or money. He said, "Maybe I can get him to break the rules."

"Try."

"In putting out those arrows," Apple told the little
man after a fast think, "you contravened Section D,
Rule 404, of the Highway Code."

"I didn't put them out. I picked them up."

"That's right. You're an accessory after the fact.
You only get six months for that. Lucky you."

"Rubbish," the rally official said weakly, raising a
hand to his alleged goatee.

"But if the witness says he didn't actually see you
do it, there's light at the tunnel's end. All you'd have
to do is get him away from here before he changes his
mind."

"Who is this witness?"

Once they were on the road it didn't take long for
Apple to explain the true circumstances, get his
chauffeur to accept that he was new BOVA member
Appleton Porter, who had been robbed.

"I *did* see a naked man holding . . . ," the rally
official said, excitedly. His manner continued similar
while Apple, as requested, went through the whole
adventure again, though keeping his story the same as
that given to the police.

His nonmention of Prunella Apple could have seen
as due to not wishing to appear a fool, the dupe, or to
the natural inclination of a gallant, so chose to believe
it was because the lady had to be significant to the
caper.

With narrowed eyes the chauffeur talked of those
other acts of sabotage. As with all members of frail
collectives, he wanted his participation repaid with
the drama that would raise the club's level of consequence.

"It's my private opinion, Porter," he said, "that the
saboteurs could belong to that riffraffy LAMA."

Although not wishing to encourage bad feeling toward the London Association of Mature Automobiles, Apple as Agent One said, "You might have something there."

"Tell you what, we'll call ahead to the hotel, see if your car's shown up."

At the same junction where they stopped to collect an arrow there was a telephone box. Into it bustled the official, who, Apple knew, cared nothing for Ethel (except insofar as he would have been disappointed if she had shown, drama over), but craved to be first to break the news of the theft.

On his return he was again excited. Apple wasn't going to believe this. Whatever next. Good heavens.

When at length, regretfully, the chauffeur relinquished his power, Apple learned that Enrico Balto's car had been totally disabled by the removal of its carburetor.

"I don't believe it."

"True true," the man said, goatee adither. "It's being towed to a city."

"Good heavens," Apple said. "And what of Enrico himself?"

"He's continuing, in good old BOVA fashion. One would almost think he had been a member for years."

"Whatever next."

"A Council of War, that's what."

Most everyone was at the hotel and in evidence when they arrived. Adele Pringle had been collecting clothes and Mavis Whittington had been collecting money. Apple was loaned jeans, shirt, sweater, socks and carpet slippers, given an envelope containing one hundred pounds, cheered for his decision to continue with the rally.

By the clothing Apple was touched, by the money

moved. As he hurried to his allotted room to change
he sweated guilt for his phoniness, presenting himself to these people as just another decent steady car-
fanatic. While showering, however, he managed to
change his feelings to pride: all this just went to show
how convincingly he had played his role.

Apple was on his way to the bar for the Council of
War when he met Prunella. "There you are," she
said, grabbing him by the biceps. "What *is* this about
you being robbed?"

Apple watched her carefully during his relating of
the true story. Her concern and surprise seemed genuine, as did her, "I only know that you fell asleep.
Aware of what a hard day you'd had yesterday, I let
you sleep on, leaving quietly."

Apple said, "I think somebody doped the tea while
we were strolling."

"Who?"

"LAMA, people're saying." He offered thanks to
the luck he had been born with that Prunella hadn't
seen him in the leather overcoat; then to his ingenu-
ity for the way it had shown him how to get the
buttons undone with a coat-hanger.

"But it'll be terrible if something's happened to
Ethel."

"Let's go to the war dance."

In the crowded bar half the people were trying to
bring peace, the other half were telling them to be
quiet. Enrico Balto stood humbly and retiringly in a
prominent position. Stroking his Zapata moustache,
Jacob Planter looked as though he considered himself
to be among a blunder of morons. Henry Caption
was telling anyone who would listen that it might be
an idea to call the rally off before something desper-
ate happened.

Apple stood at the crowd's rear with Prunella, against whom he gently bumped on occasion. He had the bottoms of his jeans tucked into the purple socks rather than have cuffs six inches above his ankles.

Apple felt that Prunella was innocent—unless, of course, she'd had training in how to speak and act a lie, the way operatives had; but that, he knew, couldn't be because such courses were available only in the secret services.

With order restored, in a manner of many speaking, the Council opened. Everyone had something to say, even if it was only "Nonsense." When a vote on whether to continue to Vienna was taken, all hands were raised in a yea and a fair proportion of them were clenched. There was heavy avoidance of the term "newcomers."

Dr. Whittington, when she was given the floor by the three people who, unbeknown to each other, were acting as chairman, said, "I propose a watch on the vehicles. At all times."

After everybody had done telling his neighbour that what the doctor had proposed was a watch on the vehicles, at all times, a vote was taken on the matter. Yeas winning, it was decided that at dinner there would be a double lottery, one to pick the first four watchers for the graveyard shift.

People began to drift out to the lobby, Apple included. He was still there half an hour later, telling his story for the ninth time (in picnic-with-Prunella truth), while she herself stood nearby telling others of her close connexion with the outrage.

Jacob Planter came to hover and make signs at Apple, who at last gave up pretending not to notice. He got away. The inventor told him:

"Whoever took your jalopy must've made an effort to hide it where it wasn't too hard to find."

"What does that mean?"

"The cops have it. They just called. It's on its way here, being driven in relays from one police district to the next."

The charge of joy that ran up through Apple he expressed in suitable Anglo-Saxon fashion, by fondly smiling. He said, "Oh, good." But he was so happy with the news that his subservience to the mores didn't deliver its usual shaft of disgust. In fact, he allowed his smile to blossom.

"Knew you'd be delirious," Jacob Planter said like a sneer, moving away.

Prunella, although she bubbled at the news, did pout, "Now you can't be my co-pilot."

"Why don't you be mine?"

"No, I must drive to the end myself."

Calling the original police office to thank them, Apple learned that their find was accidental. Ethel, with all his property intact, keys in the ignition, had been put into a barn which the farmer used once a month. His sole reason for today's unusual visit was to be alone with one of his female workers, who had suddenly become amorous.

Apple mused that although the saboteur had meant Ethel no harm, he certainly hadn't intended that she should be found until the rally was finished.

When the reunion with Ethel was over and she had been examined for signs of damage, and the police had gone, taking the leather coat, Apple changed again, putting on his dinner jacket. The borrowed clothes he returned item by item to their owners. The money he gave to BOVA's Hon Sec, to be used for extra wine at the gala dinner on the last night beyond Vienna.

With others, Apple began meandering into the dining room, where he had arranged to sit with Prunella. At a call from behind he turned. Adele Pringle bustled up like a small tank.

Shooting cigarette ash she said, "I do wish you'd help Enrico out. He has almost no German and he'll probably say the wrong thing."

"To whom?"

"The reporter. He heard about the sabotage to Enrico's car. This is the last thing the rally needs."

"But maybe the first that Balto needs."

"I hope you're not suggesting he disabled his car himself."

"You never know with that class of people."

The poet had a good cough before saying with grind, "Enrico Balto, Alias Witherspoon, comes from a perfectly sound working-class family, I'll have you know."

"I do know."

"Salt of the earth."

"The class I was referring to, Pring, wasn't social. I meant people in show business. Promotion is an essential part of their trade, naturally enough."

They were interrupted by the official who had been Apple's chauffeur. He said, "Mr. Balto is—"

"I'm coming."

Singer and reporter were in a corner of the lobby. Apple introduced himself in German as the association's unofficial interpreter.

Balto said, "I have been endeavouring to explain that this could have been the work of a rival at the Metropolitan."

"The Metropolitan, an insurance company, has no

rival in this kind of work," Apple told the raincoated man whose hatbrim, if not quite turned up at the front, was straight enough to want to be.

"But I have to change for dinner," Enrico Balto said. "I wouldn't want to be photographed like this anyway. Ask him to wait half an hour for the whole story."

Singer gone, Apple said, "There's been some confusion, I'm afraid. The old language barrier. Insurance was referred to because Mr. Balto wants his expenses paid for: he had to remove his carburetor because of malfunction. There's no news item."

The reporter frowned with suspicion, as though he had been congratulated on his decency. He said, "When people claim there's no news item, there generally is."

"You see right through me," Apple confessed with a shucks sway. "There's no fooling a real pro boy like you."

Suspicion lost: "Go on, sir."

"But the item's nothing to do with Balto's car. That's a red herring. He wants you to meet him here in an hour, by the way, so he can show baby photographs and tell you his life story."

"Forget it," the reporter said. "What's the item?"

Voice low, Apple told of the scoop he could give the pro boy if he maintained a low profile. He couldn't go into detail. But it was hot. Hottest Common Market foul-up for years.

"It's up to you if you hang around or not," Apple said. "All that can happen is, One, it might stop the item from happening, and, Two, *Der Spiegel* is sure to hear about it—and your scoop has flown."

Apple left the man with his telephone number and his acceptance apparently solid, built by a clincher of vanity: that the only thing he asked in exchange for the scoop was that he be named as the most significant personage in the item's disclosure. As Apple knew, a priestly virtue may sometimes be doubted, a cardinal sin never.

Dinner passed pleasantly with Prunella shimmering in a silver dress whose cleavage showed where her breastbone ended, proudly, as though it were a rainbow. In the candlelight she looked like the product of a dream. That she was real, however, which Apple both forgave and enjoyed, came with her admission that her shoes were killing her.

The lotteries came and went. With the new draw, Apple was relieved not to be one of tonight's watchers. He was looking forward to his bed, which embarrassed him but didn't stop him.

Prunella agreed to meet Apple in the bar for a nightcap when she returned from changing her shoes. Apple entered the bar at a stroll. In his tuxedo he felt very James Bond. If he had known how to make a martini he would have told the barman how he wanted his martini made.

Through the window Apple looked over the parking area, seen as a dim collection of car roofs getting dimmer the further they spread from the hotel's lights.

To Apple it occurred that, as the watch hadn't begun yet, stupidly, this would be a perfect time to do a bit of sabotage. Which made him realise that the same thought could have occurred to someone else, and in respect of Ethel.

Apple strode out of the bar and over to the entrance. Outside he wended swiftly between parked vehicles. When he heard a step behind him he thought nothing of it; and when the footsteps closed in and a hand gripped his elbow he thought he was about to be challenged by an early, zealous watcher. A voice said in German, "Just keep walking, Herr Porter."

FOUR

The car, parked on the road's edge, was a big black Mercedes. Apple was eased into its back by the man who had stayed behind him, unseen, and who followed him inside. Door closed, the car moved off in a hasteless glide. The front held two silent, still men with necks as broad as their heads.

That Apple had made no fuss about being marched off, not even a verbal complaint, was on account of the elbow-grip which his companion now ended.

Apple knew that grip. Through nerve pressure it created a grizzly sensation pitched between pain and severe pins-and-needles, rendering the body malleable and the mind numb. During practice sessions at Damian House Apple had managed to get precisely the right spot only once in every three tries, though somehow when it was his turn to play victim the gripper rarely failed.

Apple swung his head to the man in a dislike that was no act. He asked, "What the hell is all this?" He spoke autocratic German.

"You will find out in a few minutes, Herr Porter," the man said, still granite polite, the firing-squad captain. Feedback from the headlights showed a standard hard-guy face complete with scarred chin.

Someone's deliveryman, Apple decided as he said, "I insist on being told what's going on here."

The man said nothing. One of the pair in front sniffed, a sound more homey than sinister.

Apple: "If you lot are with that other old-car club . . ." They were with another club, he knew, the way a male could be with child.

The man continuing silent Apple asked, "Who are you? Where are you taking me?"

"I would advise you," the man said, "to save your questions." It could have meant *I have no answers,* or *I'm not allowed to discuss this,* or *If you go on talking I'll break your leg.*

Facing front Apple folded his arms viciously, a brat who can't have his own way. "We'll see," he mumbled.

The man agreed, "We will."

The rival-club offering had been right, Apple told himself. He had to give them something they thought he believed, so they wouldn't suspect he had them figured as possible secret service personnel, which figuring they would know could only be because he was secret service himself.

After a two-minute silence for the dead he could be if he played the scene wrong, the car duringly going along a deserted country road, Apple said:

"At least tell me if you people were responsible for stealing my car today." It wasn't a solution he was all that interested in, he wanted to hear more of the man's speech to see what nationality he could read in it.

Although the man said nothing, his leg twitched, which might have been an answer of the admission type, Apple felt. He didn't try for more talk.

Another ten minutes and they turned through a farm gateway. The track of mud soon brought into view a small manor house, lights pinking prettily in many of its windows as though it were posing for a Christmas card or trying to look benign.

As the car stopped out front, the broad door swung inwards to display the silhouette of a man. That he was no butler showed in his colonel stance. When Apple was alighting from the car he turned away with, "Come along in, Herr Porter."

The room Apple followed into was as cozy as the exterior promise, with low beams carved and painted, chintzy furniture and a giant's yawn hearth in which a log fire smiled. The door closed behind him.

"Please sit down," the host said, bowing toward an armchair as though he considered any form of pointing to be bad manners. "What can I get you to drink?"

"Nothing."

"Quite sure, Herr Porter?"

"Quite, quite sure," Apple said, sitting. "Unless explanations come in glasses."

"How witty," the man said. "I do like the English sense of humour." Fifty, he was as handsome and well-groomed as an actor who had married money, his dinner jacket a gem of understated quality, his face mellow from its latest massage, his grey hair wiggish. He wore a pleasant expression.

Apple asked, "How do you feel about the English sense of fair play?"

Still standing on the hearth rug the host said after a more-in-sorrow wince, "Please don't be antagonistic, Herr Porter. It won't help. I do apologise for this, sincerely, and I promise you my intentions are honourable."

"You have abducted me. You have committed an offence against me both immoral and criminal. You have deprived me of my liberty. You are subjecting me to emotional stress."

"Well, yes."

"I demand an explanation, an apology and my immediate release," Apple said. "Whether or not I report you and your henchmen to the authorities is my business. A lot will depend on the nature of your explanation."

"Herr Porter," the host began in a comfortable manner. He didn't go on until he was sitting nearby, on the arm of a couch, and that he was thus maintaining the psychological advantage of superior physical position Apple didn't miss.

"Let me tell you about the organization to which I belong. It has to do with international relations. Our aims, if you'll forgive my lack of modesty, are high."

"I can forgive anything but verbosity."

"Sorry. In short, my colleagues and I are dedicated to world peace."

"How unusual. How strange."

"Please, Herr Porter. We are very serious, very private and discreet, we finance operations ourselves, we are of several nationalities."

Apple said, "I'm still waiting for the explanation of why I have been taken prisoner."

"I thought this would be the best way for us to have a sincere talk, you and I."

"About what?"

"You, Herr Porter. Your intentions."

Flatly Apple said, "I don't understand."

The man nodded. "Perhaps you don't," he said. "But it is curious that as soon as you join the British Old Vehicles Association you come on this rally."

"I joined BOVA months ago."

"There seems to be something a little odd about that as well. A slice of circumstantial evidence."

"This is all gibberish."

The man said, "And you do appear to be determined to carry on with the rally to the bitter end."

"Nothing wrong with that," Apple said.

"Which bitter end, I'm sure I don't need to tell you, lies close to the Czech border."

"Your point being?"

"Come now, Herr Porter," the host said, eyes kindly. "You are a skilled linguist, a top man in your field. Certainly you represent an excellent catch in the realm of defection. And it occurred to us that you might be planning to do just that, slip behind the Iron Curtain."

Apple had no need to act surprised. He gaped like an angler who, living a cartoon cliché, reels in a boot. Next he gave way to the absurdity of it all and splurged into laughter. Had the circumstances been different he would have slapped the host's shoulder to show appreciation of his being a card, a wag and a one.

But the man was serious, so much so that he was able to smile tolerantly at the guest's mirth and ask, "Would you like that drink now, Herr Porter?"

"Sure," Apple said around a chortle. "Sherry on the rocks. I haven't heard anything so ridiculous for years. Hilarious idea."

"You can prove it is?"

"I'll say I can."

The host had moved over to a cocktail cabinet, where he asked, "How?"

"Well," Apple said. "Um." That was as far as he got. However, by the time he had his drink and the

man was sitting again, whiskey in hand, he had a list
ready.

"I have my job waiting. I have my flat and my
country cottage. I have my friends and my car. I have
my dog. I have my healthy bank account. Those are
the majors. If I'd been planning to defect I would've
made certain arrangements."

"Which might have given the show away."

"No, really. The idea's ridiculous."

"Nevertheless," the host said, "we are taking it seriously. Your health."

"Cheers," Apple said. He had to admit that sitting
here, with a drink, by a fire, in his tuxedo, he felt
highly civilised. After sipping he asked, "What about
the other new BOVA members and defection?"

"They're of minor consequence. They couldn't be
built up as strongly in the valuable-asset sense as
yourself by the Soviet press. It, apart from overstat-
ing your respectability, would represent you as being
in possession of much sensitive knowledge."

Apple said, "Hardly."

"You must have done government work as a trans-
lator during your years at the United Kingdom
Philological Institute. Also, weren't you an interpreter at that NATO meeting in Madrid two months
ago?"

"Government work, no. And every subject brought
out at the Madrid session was made public."

The host said, "That's the most suspicious thing
you've said yet."

Apple busily swirled the ice in his glass. "Look
here, what exactly do you want? Shall I give you my
word I'm not planning to defect?"

"If you were planning defection, Herr Porter, you

would be a turncoat, therefore your word would obviously be useless."

"Then what's the next step?"

Cozily, like a grandfather beginning a once-upon-a-time, the host said, "What we're going to do is let you stay on here with us for a few days. It's to protect you. It's to give you time to think, to ponder thoroughly your future, with no outside influences."

"Keep me here?" Apple asked, a high edge of nervousness in his voice.

"Allow me to show you something, Herr Porter. Bring your drink, if you wish."

They went through a door, along a passage and into a bed-sitting room, It looked to be typical guest quarters, with a bathroom attached, with all the comforts, with radio and books and television. Table lamps gave a soft, friendly glow.

"If, in a few days, you're still determined to defect," the host said, "naturally we will let you leave. We're only trying to help."

"What was it you were going to show me?"

Neatly, going out: "Your room." The door closed.

Apple didn't waste his time seeing if it was locked. In a daze born of a refusal to accept that if the situation persisted Agent One's caper was finished, he put his glass down and went to the window.

Drawing heavy drapes aside Apple saw that, although there were no bars, beyond the glass was a shutter. Solid, not in slats, it looked vault-strong.

In any case, Apple was starting to understand the thoroughness involved here. Even if he wasn't being watched via some Judas-hole or hidden camera, the room was sure to be bugged with the care of a nursery, meaning that investigation would immediately follow any untoward noise—such as that caused by a guest trying to batter his way out with a piece of furniture.

Bathroom offering no hope of an exit, Apple began to pace by the bedfoot. His daze gradually cleared, allowing him to see with clarity the caper's possible death. It made little difference whether the host was what he claimed to be, doing what he claimed to be doing, silly though that story sounded (odd-ball groups did exist), or if he was KGB with orders to keep away from the rally anyone who could possibly interfere with Defector's plans.

Apple went to the door. Pounding on it he shouted a tirade about his respectability, his loyalty to his country, his intentions of seeing that the host would pay for this outrage to the last letter of the law, his need of a toothbrush.

Silent again, he listened. There was no response.

Tedious in mind Apple went to the bed and lay down. He gained a smidgen of ugly relief from not taking his shoes off. Eyes closed, he relaxed. He allowed himself to start drifting along the shores of sleep.

Monico opened his mouth and knocked. Knowing that dogs didn't make noises like that, they barked, Apple struggled out of the dream.

At another knock he sat up and called out, "Enter." A look at his watch told him he had slept for hours. It was two o'clock in the morning.

Deliveryman came in. His demeanor amiable, his tough face affable, he said in an English which had started with mother's milk, "Come along, Mr. Porter. You're leaving now."

Apple got off the bed. "About time."

"Have you got everything?" the man asked, patting himself the way people do.

"Yes," Apple said, patting himself also, the way people do also.

"If you'd care to follow me, please."

They went out of the room and to the passage end, through a door and into the night, around to the house front and over to a car.

Its driver Apple didn't know, its single rear passenger he did. Getting in the back he said, "Good morning, sir."

After a fast start the car had reduced speed. This was due to Angus Watkin having used a microphone to tell the driver, separated by a glass panel, that they were not, as it happened, in any particular hurry—a Watkinism for *Slow down, idiot.*

Apple was pleased with himself for having shown no surprise at seeing his Control in the car, even though this was more on account of doziness than decision, and despite his knowing that the reverse had been wanted by Watkin. Apple saw no reason to pamper his chief's ego at the moment. He was feeling used and abused.

Furthermore, he would be damned if he would be the first to speak, Apple assured himself with a lifted top lip just before he said, "What a surprise."

Angus Watkin shuffled. It was like a house settling for the night. He asked, "My presence or the fact that your captors aren't what they seem to be?"

"Both, sir. Though I do know you get about a bit."

"It's broadening, I'm told."

"And I suppose it's safe to assume my hosts aren't KGB."

"It is, sadly," Angus Watkin said. "Be more interesting if they were."

"They're just a bunch of crazies, then?"

"That, Porter, is not for me to say."

"I understand."

"Since you certainly do not, I'll tell you. They are DG7, which is a department of British Intelligence. Its duties spread in many directions and it is noted for three factors: eccentric schemes, incompetence, and being something of a nuisance to its betters."

After absorbing that Apple said, "So it was through the service connexion, sir, that you found out they had me."

"No, Porter. Connexions with DG7 are, fortunately, meagre. I heard through our German friends, who seem to be keeping an eye on the rally."

"Must be someone I know, then."

"That's neither here nor there," Angus Watkin said. "And as to DG7, they would no more tell me anything than I would give them the right time in Greenwich."

Which statement was strong stuff for his Control, Apple well knew. This man's miffed comment was another man's snarled outburst.

"Nor, Porter, is tonight's debacle the first time DG7 has stepped wobblingly onto my territory. One can hardly hope that it will be the last."

Unaware of the cheeriness which instinct put into his voice to counter, ease, a hint of despondency in his companion, Apple said, "So they had to be told I was an Upstairs operative."

Angus Watkin said, "I would as soon uncover one of my people to those amateurs as I would my neck to the sword."

"Course not. Silly of me."

"I said you had become a useful red herring and should be let alone."

"You told them I was innocent."

"I told them you were mad."

Weakly: "Neat idea."

"I said you were certifiably insane and if there were such a thing as defection in your addled head it would be good news for the West."

"Did they swallow it, sir?" Apple asked as though ready to be astounded at an affirmative.

"With the necessary coupling that the reason you were on the rally was that you were in love with one of the competitors, Dr. Mavis Whittington."

Sourly: "Neatish."

"And the reason they accepted that was because I told them about your mother complex, among other problems, including your obsessive belief that sherry is poison unless mixed with ice."

Taking pleasure from that last verb being certainly wrong, Apple said, "Well done."

"Whether or not those latter statements of mine hold any truth I do not know, Porter. The first, obviously, is a lie."

Not knowing if he ought to laugh at what might be an attempt at humour, feel offended at what was patently an insult, or try to figure out what his chief was talking about lastly, Apple indulged in a bout of coughing. It was that pathetic sound often made by people who have been imprisoned.

Unmoved, Angus Watkin said, "The truth of the matter is that you appear to be somewhat enamoured of another of our Possibles—Prunella Bank."

"Oh no, sir," Apple said. "I never mix business with pleasure. My interest in the young lady is related strictly to the mission."

"I must remind you, Porter, that a certain state of nudity has been mentioned."

"Ms. Bank wasn't even there at that particular

time." He went on to describe the incident, being honest except for the details about which he lied.

The car was approaching the hotel. Using the microphone Angus Watkin told the driver to stop in the roadside before getting too close. To Apple he said:

"My motivation in coming to Germany in person rather than send an emissary, was, first, to enjoy a jolly chat with the DG7 people, and second, to contiguously get from you a progress report on the operation."

"Yes, sir."

"All the progress, however," Angus Watkin said, "seems to have been made not by Agent One but by a person or persons unknown. You, in short, have had more problems than all the Possibles combined."

With a victim whine in his voice Apple said, "Looks to me as though I've been ganged up on, sir. What with DG7 and maybe KGB and maybe even the German lot and rival car clubs and older members of BOVA."

The car drew to a stop. Watkin asked, "No one else?"

Ignoringly: "On my side, I've been far from idle. It's been go go go. And I've completely disabled Enrico Balto's car. It's out."

"But its owner isn't."

"He won't be able to make a dash for the border unless he steals someone else's car."

"The crossing will be made clandestinely, on foot, not frontally at a checkpoint."

Stubborn, Apple said, "He'll still need a vehicle of some kind to get there and I can be on the lookout for that."

From Angus Watkin came a sound that could have been a sigh. "There isn't much time left, Porter," he said. "The night after tomorrow you rally people will be at the last hotel."

"True, sir."

"However, if you don't succeed, you don't succeed. It would be rather a pity if DG7 did."

Which Apple read as a ranted confession that his chief would sooner the world came to an end in two days than have the DG7 people best him in the mission.

Angus Watkin turned to look at Apple squarely. Any other spymaster might have glared, lifted a fist, worked jaw muscles or grimly wished his underling luck. Watkin said a mild "Good morning, Porter."

As Apple, walking by the light of a near-full moon, was drawing closer to the white fence that separated hotel parking from road, he heard from among the vehicles a low voice. That he was able to hear was due to him walking on the road's sandy shoulder.

Another voice answered the first. Apple went at a slower and started to stoop. He had reached a low crouch by the time he was near where the first voice had come from, where cars were backed up against the fence, and where he almost fell over with shock.

The two beams of light caught him in their cross-fire. A voice next shouted harshly, "Don't move."

Apple disobeyed. But slowly. As he creaked erect, blind to everything in the flashlights' glare, he managed a huffed "What's going on here?" He was rattled even though he realised he had only fallen afoul of the nightwatch.

"It's Appleton Porter," said the first voice, which belonged to Henry Caption. "Well well."

The other voice, belonging to a rally member, said, "What an interesting catch."

Apple, holding his hands up to fend off the glare:
"If you wouldn't mind, friends."

"Friends, eh? Well well."

The member asked a brutal, "What're you doing
sneaking around here, Porter?"

"Sneaking? I? *Sneaking?* I'm on my way back from a
stroll, I'll have you know."

"It's getting along for three in the morning."

"Wonderful," Apple said. "Now I'll be able to
sleep."

Reluctantly, the flashlights sank from his face.
Henry Caption said, "You could've been up to something shady, it seems to me."

"Down to something, perhaps you mean. What I
was doing was seeing if I could slip close to whom-
ever it was I could hear whispering. I thought it had
to be you nightwatchers, but I wasn't taking any
chances."

The member said, in hope, "How do we know he's
not causing a diversion?"

Henry Caption, visible now, turned his head to
call, "All right over there?"

Two people called back to say no, they were freezing cold as well as dying of boredom.

As he had been trained to do in these circumstances, Apple attacked. He stepped to the fence and
lifted his leg over while saying, loud and bluff:

"You're alert enough, friends, I'll say that for you.
But what's needed here is a little more organization.
Now when I was with the Civil Defence . . ."

He went on telling about what he had once seen in
a television documentary as he walked between the
two cars which separated the men, one of whom
grumbled that this would have to be reported to the
Committee anyway. Henry Caption followed behind.

He said, "You must admit your behaviour's been odd."

In French Apple said, "So has yours."

"*Mai . . . ,*" began the ex-runner, then switched back to English for, "What're you playing at?" He laughed. "Language games?" He laughed again. "Anything to change the subject?"

"Sounds as though your French isn't bad."

"If twenty words isn't bad—great."

"You'll excuse me if I don't stay and barter values," Apple said, striding on. "My stroll's got me in the perfect mood for sleep. Good night."

"Prunella waited nearly an hour for you in the bar," Henry Caption said, "Good night."

With no more sounds of pursuit Apple went on and into the slumbering hotel. Up in his room he found a note; it had been slid under the door. Signed with a P, it asked, *Where are you?*

Relieved to discover that he was too tired to be interested at the moment in feeling flattered, which would start him on a neurotic binge about being vain, which he was sure he wasn't, Apple quickly undressed. He was falling asleep even before his head hit the pillow.

If barking dogs don't bite do knocking dogs not enter?—Apple wondered as he realised he was in that same dream again, the only difference being that this time the one talking knocks was Prunella, whom he had just finished pelting with pebbles. They had been through this before, Apple thought while the picture started to disintegrate at the interruption of a voice: "This is the last call. You won't get another."

Apple came fully awake. His watch told him he was late. Leaping out of bed he began on a graceless assault on the necessaries—ablutions, dressing, breakfast. The last, brought in from where it had been left outside the door, consisted of brown bread and sausage and now-cold coffee.

Going downstairs and outdoors Apple saw that, as expected, he had long missed his turn. Instead of being in the middle he was three from the last.

Forgetting to hide his indifference, whistling as he drew up to the line, he caused the starter to quiver an unspoken accusation of not taking the serious things of life seriously. Apple, silent, did a spell of hand-wringing to show that with his whistling he hadn't managed to hide from himself the hurt he was feeling at missing his place. The starter told him he had to learn to take the rough with the smooth.

A drizzle came on once Apple got settled to the road. He went at a leisurely pace which he thought of as being because the tarmac was slick rather than admit that Ethel's ancient window-wiper was less than efficient.

The three last cars in the run Apple let go on past. He felt easy. Despite being leaned on by a Control whose grim concern was more for personal face than national, having at least one rival, plus a German observer, he knew that right now there was nothing he could accomplish. He still had forty-eight hours. He was no more worried about the caper than he was over having stood Prunella up.

Following an uneventful morning, Apple had seventeen stories prepared to explain his absence last night. Hastily he tried to select a winner when he came in sight of a lunch stop, among whose several rally cars was a prewar Buick. Story Number Three, he crowned, entering the cafeteria.

At one large table were a dozen BOVA members, including Mavis Whittington, Jacob Planter and Prunella Bank. Being that the table was for twelve, when Apple got there with his tray people had to shift chairs, though Prunella made no effort to create a space between herself and a young male rallier at one side and Planter at the other. She did, however, smile, in a vapours sort of way, on Apple telling her he could explain.

After some serio-comic joshing of the newcomer over his nocturnal doings with the watchers had faded, he started to eat, which, since he was the only one still eating, he did shrinkingly, feeling remiss. He listened as the talk returned to what, his neighbour filled in, had been suggested prior to his arrival: that they all stick together on the road, for protection.

Everyone was noisy, vying to be more in favour of the suggestion than anybody else. They got rumpled in agreement. They looked from face to face but couldn't find someone to convince. At the vote they each said so many ayes so passionately it sounded like a hundred sailors taking orders to break out the rum.

A man got up. "Okay," he said. "Let's go." Everybody began to move and another man called out, "Wagons, roll!"

Apple, wishing he could think of things like that to say, gobbled at his stew. Most of it he left but he was still last outside. Bustling, he caught Prunella as she was about to drive off. He offered Number Three.

Looking up at him through the window she said, "If you'd wanted to keep your own personal vigil on the cars you could have waited till tonight. It's your turn."

"I was worried about the Buick, actually."

"And if you did leave a note with the bartender I didn't get it."

"Well . . ."

"Now, please, Apple," Prunella said, revving. "I must be moving." She shot away.

With cars shunting and horns blasting Apple plodded to Ethel. He told himself everything was fine. He didn't feel at all guilty. It was nothing to worry about. Ever since inns and pubs began, people had been putting blame on bartenders.

Apple yawned. The spasm came not from tiredness but nerves, he recognised. Here it was midafternoon already, the hours flitting past like birds late home, and no progress whatever had been made—except by Defector, who was getting ever closer to his destination.

Matters were worsened for Apple by the motorcade's pace, which was being set at a spanking dirge by the leader. Dr. Mavis Whittington drove her little blue MG as though she were afraid of disturbing whatever archaeological finds might lie beneath the road.

Not for the first time, Apple considered passing the caravan and leaving it behind. As before, what stopped him was having no ideas as to what he would do then; or so he guessed, avoiding that it could be because he didn't want to appear the outsider to the others, especially Prunella.

In spite of his tension, Apple couldn't help but admire the sight whenever a long, open curve obliged: a dozen codger automobiles in immaculate condition, ranging from a tiny Fiat to the big Buick, from a cheap Austin 7 to Jacob Planter's luxury Cord convertible.

Buildings appeared. Modern, they formed a town's outer suburb, with businesses standing back from the road, wide here. Apple nodded approval as Dr. Whittington led her followers to a trickly halt.

There were two places offering refreshments/restrooms. The debate over which to patronise was in full fume when Apple reached the frontward assembly, after taking care to lock Ethel. Some people were for the closest, which was indoors, some for the terrace café farther along where parking was out but from where the cars could be watched.

A woman, eyes canny, suggested the posting of guards, if the closest was to be used. A man asked for volunteers. When everyone had stopped looking at everyone else, the woman broke the silence: "To the terrace we go."

It was a quarter hour before they were settled and served, at three adjoining tables. Apple, outskirmished, got left off the table Prunella and Jacob Planter shared with another couple. He sipped his pop aggressively.

In among the talk of the place they would stay at tonight, this side of Passau, and of tomorrow's crossing into Austria, and whether or not it was going to rain again, there were running comments on the motorcade's audience. As always, the old cars had attracted a collection of admirers, prompting:

"That rotten little boy's going to climb right on top of my Sarah any minute."

"If we had the time I'd offer to give those girls a spin."

"That official is such a nosy sod."

"I bet the old boy there had a Fiat like yours once."

"If only they'd keep their hands off."

"I could've sworn the official passed us ten minutes ago, after that last arrow."

"No, I don't think he did."

Looking away from where Jacob Planter had his arm on the back of Prunella's chair, looking toward the cars, Apple saw a figure in knee-length dustcoat and billowy cap. The ensemble goggles were over the eyes, which alerted Apple more than his vague recollection that the dustcoat should reach down to the ankles.

One of the ralliers said, "For two pins the sod would climb right inside."

The man was leaning in under the black canvas top of the first car. Mavis Whittington asked, "What the devil can he be looking at?"

That Apple didn't say he thought the man could be an imposter was because he might turn out to be one of the other officials and Apple would look stupid, the raw neophyte. He still didn't speak out when the man, his movements swift, got into the MG's driving seat.

Everyone gasped and nattered. Mavis Whittington rumbled, "What a bloody cheek."

"Wait a second," Jacob Planter said in the drawl of a suspicion floating down to its feet. "That guy is a phony."

Apple snapped "Yes an imposter I knew it I knew it all along" was buried under the clamour that suddenly arose as came the sound of the MG being started.

Next, it shot forward.

"Help!" Dr. Whittington cried.

Her car came on. It went past the terrace while the ralliers were still trying to get out of each other's way.

Apple got clear. He reached level ground and shouted back, "I'll catch him."

Appearing beside him Jacob Planter laughed. He said, "In that crate of yours?"

They ran on toward the motorcade, with others tumulting behind, in every voice a trill of shameful pleasure. Planter peeled off at his car and when Apple glanced back on reaching Ethel he saw that Prunella was also getting into the Cord. Other people were similarly doubling up.

Apple dropped his keys. This was due to his being supercareful about not dropping his keys. By the time he was inside Ethel, sitting at the wheel and ready for off, the other pursuit cars had gone, leaving in charge of the remainder the canny suggester of guards, who held her head aslant in the style of a martyr.

Apple pulled away fast. He groaned on seeing by the terrace café a menace. Mavis Whittington was gesturing forcefully to be given a lift. The stop and pick-up would gobble many valuable seconds.

Apple quickly toyed with the scheme of pretending not to notice, of looking the other way as he had done when passing the guard or of peering at the dashboard. Dr. Whittington's expression of panic and anxiety made him put that toy away, sigh and come to a vicious halt.

Opening the door, the archaeologist started to creak heftily into the back. She panted, "They wouldn't stop, the others, cos they know I hate speed."

"Yes yes. Get in."

"You'll go nice and steadily, of course."

"Yes yes yes. Get in."

"You're the steady type, young Appleton," Mavis Whittington said. "It's written all over you."

Reaching an arm out and backwards, Apple

slammed the door as soon as he could no longer bear
not doing so, giving the doctor merely a small, helpful clout on her rump. The way he spurted off fast
was also an aid, he told himself, in that it showed the
passenger where to sit.

When she had finished wrestling with herself to get
around the proper way from her fall onto the seat,
Mavis Whittington asked, "You're not picking up
speed, are you?"

With his head to the side Apple shouted through
the open sliding-glass panel behind him that he
couldn't hear a word. He kept his foot down on the
power and ignored his passenger when she called out
again.

Neither her speed preferences nor her car were of
any more interest to Apple at this moment than was
the mission. He had become the boy whose best girl
was being given a ride on that sneery kid's new bike.

Scanning about keenly as, on leaving the suburb,
they topped a rise, Apple saw the chase. Across fields,
six cars were visible, the first well ahead of Number
Two, Planter's Cord, which was leading by several
lengths from the remainder of the pack.

Going down the rise Apple let Ethel have her head.
She responded like a flirt to a wink. Apple grinned in
doubt as her chassis clanked, her front wheels shim-
mied and her body's every part except the most intimate squeaked or rattled or groaned, all to the elegy
of Dr. Whittington's loud protests.

Yet Apple persisted. He felt sure Ethel could with-
stand the treatment. After all, she had been receiving
for years the finest of care from the best specialists in
London. But, came the niggle, had she gone soft?

Apple saw the side road where the chase must have

turned off. Slowing down enough to be noticed by an expert he cut over to form a wide arc. He made the turn accompanied by a new loud thud from behind, which he knew could only have been his passenger falling over, so didn't give himself the trouble of checking in the rear-view.

He did slip a fast hand back to slide the panel shut. It was just in time. The doctor's grinding shouts, though not intelligible behind glass and racket, had an intimation of grossness.

Thrillingly, the tail car came into view. Trembling no less than Ethel herself, Apple began to blow the horn as he drew closer. The stunted Fiat, with three people aboard, started hugging the inside of the two-lane byway. Apple slipped past with a final beep of thanks.

The road wound on under heavy trees. Bends forced Ethel to slow, which reduced body and wind noise, which enabled Apple to hear when his passenger yelled that she would come there and tell him.

In the mirror he saw her pulling herself forward. He gave Ethel a little spurt. Feet lifting, the doctor sank back. She recovered and tried again, and again was sent gently back with a spurt.

This continued, with Apple not disenjoying his power but trying not to get too involved in the poignant way Dr. Whittington described little circles with her arms.

Around the last bend of the series, speeding up, Apple came on another car. He closed the gap fast, with hornplay. But the driver of the ancient Morris, a retired right-wing politician, seemed to find the middle of the road intriguing.

The pace he was reduced to when he had drawn within a metre of the Morris was painful for Apple.

He yelled with his head out of the window as well as blasting his horn in staccato. The Morris stayed complacently central.

On coming back inside Apple saw danger: Mavis Whittington was up on her feet and reaching for the panel. His forward spurt was automatic. The doctor fell onto the seat in coincidence with the crash of Ethel's front bumper on the car in front.

The Morris swerved into the side like a skittery horse. Pulling out to pass Apple mused a tough *That's the way to show the bastards.* He tingled at his implacability and brute style.

Affecting not to notice the driver and co-pilot's rightish glares and raised fists, Apple went on by. He let Ethel charge forward. Mavis Whittington, he noted, was holding on to the straps at either side.

Driving at risk, Apple soon caught up with the next car. He was about to start on his horn demands when he needed to brake hard: the Citroën in front had made a sudden turn through a gateway.

Not having gone past, Apple fought the steering-wheel around and followed. He came into a field. It was large, spreading beyond view over a low, graceful crest, topping which was the blue MG. Jacob Planter's Cord was ahead of the other two cars.

The field was a gift for Apple. Racing across stubble he simply made straight for the crest instead of following the tracks which curved to that point and on which the Citroën stayed.

His sole risk was in hitting his head on the roof during the excessive bouncing. In order not to see how this was being handled by the archaeologist he moved his rear-view out of position. In order not to hear same he shouted a Viking battle charge, in Norse.

He startled himself. Shout gone, he settled for a. bulldog growling.

Ethel was approaching the crest fast. All was plain sailing. Abruptly, there exploded the possibility of a head-on collision. The MG was coming back.

With mere feet to spare both drivers veered away, Apple with frantic slaps on the wheel like judo cutlets. He was no longer growling.

Continuing the circle, his droop of release bringing Ethel to a crawl, he noted that the two trailing cars had entered the field and in the corner of his eye saw the Cord flash by. He changed gear and went for speed.

On the down run Apple saw another car in his eye-corner. A full look showed him, just come over the crest, the Citroën. He shot across at top bounce and put it into fourth place.

Neat, One, Apple thought. He also mused that, since the MG's driver was heading back for the gate, he didn't know the lay of the land and so couldn't be a local man, for what that was worth.

Next, Apple opened his mouth at the scene below. Although the Morris had only slowed, now that the MG was in view, the Fiat had swung off its course. It was heading straight for Mavis Whittington's roadster.

As the two cars drew closer together, an accident seeming inevitable, Apple opened his mouth still wider and took one hand off the wheel to strainingly push air aside.

With inches to spare the MG squeaked by in front of the Fiat, which then halted, at a jerk.

Swerving, Planter's convertible went behind it. Apple was intending to do the same until he saw body language that made him change his mind.

In an older car, few people can engage reverse gear without leaning forward, unconsciously helping the hand find that difficult slot. The Fiat's driver had leaned.

Even as Apple started turning the steering-wheel the Fiat began to move backwards. He went across its front with Ethel lifted so far up that he thought she might go into a roll. The slope helped.

Correcting, Apple headed for the gate with his jaw out. Now the race was between himself and Jacob Planter.

Although narrow, the road ahead was straight. Apple realised why the MG's driver had chosen to try his luck with the field: he was aware that his blue mount probably couldn't best a Cord on a straight run, though a lot would depend on the condition of the vehicles.

And Ethel's seemed to be superb, Apple mused as he poured on the power. Already she was gaining on the Cord, even as it was gaining on the MG, whose top, round with wind like a beery belly, was creating a natural braking system.

A bus came along on the two-lane country road, sending dabs of light on the siding fences. When it had gone by Apple was shaken by a crash at the back of his head.

It was a thud on the glass panel. With a fast correction of his rear-view mirror Apple saw that Dr. Whittington, shoulders on the seat, was stretching out a battering foot.

Her face gaunt, she yelled, "Too fast!"

Uncorrecting the mirror Apple kept a grip on his sympathy by reminding himself that the archaeologist could be Defector. At a snap he switched on the radio. That what surged out was a roisterous gallop piece by Wagner didn't surprise him in the slightest.

Mavis Whittington went on with her giant tapping.

The Cord was now within two metres of the blue roadster, with Ethel double that distance back but still gaining. Apple knew he would continue to gain because the Cord daren't get any closer to the front car, which was probably flat out. They were all going in excess of eighty miles an hour.

While Jacob Planter hadn't looked around from his grim hunch at the convertible's wheel, his passenger had done so frequently. She did so again now.

Onto his face Apple clicked a jaunty expression. He turned the music louder and swept one-handed into a waft of eloquent conducting.

Prunella also gestured, though what her waves and mouthings signalled was that Apple should slow down to safety and let Jacob Planter handle this speed business, for which he had the ideal machine.

Conducting over, Apple shook his head airily. When Prunella swung around he gave his concentration to the steady, seeable gains he was making.

That lasted until silence from the panel made him use his rear-view mirror. It showed the rear compartment as being empty. Jerking his head the other way and back, Apple saw the bulk of his passenger there. Like a mountaineer traversing, Mavis Whittington had pulled herself to the door.

What's she up to?—Apple's mind gabbled. Is she going to throw herself out?

The music blasted on at full gallop, the three old cars roared along the road as though joined together, Prunella kept looking back sternly at Apple and Apple kept switching his head to check on Mavis Whittington.

This action must surely appear weird to Prunella, who couldn't see the doctor plainly, Apple realised. He wondered what he could do to render the head-switching acceptable, sane. Rub his neck? Make switches in the other direction? Pretend to be spitting out of the window?

He gave it up as, faintly, he heard a familiar squeal. Dr. Whittington was rolling down the window.

Except that he was going too fast to fool with the steering, and that his passenger would be certain to fall to the floor and hurt herself, Apple would have removed her from the door with a swerve.

With his attention divided as before he watched the window go down; watched Mavis Whittington get her head and shoulders and both arms through the space.

Next, she reached in through his window and grabbed his arm, yelling, "You didn't understand me!"

"What?" Apple shouted above the music and wind and body uproar. "What's that?" He tried to free himself so he could roll his window up.

Mavis Whittington swung her head close to bellow, "I . . . DON'T . . . LIKE . . . SPEED!"

"You don't like what?"

"SPEED!"

"Speed?"

"YES!"

Apple yelled, "Sorry. I can't go any faster."

"NO NO!"

He had lied. Ethel had a reserve.

Ahead lay a long hill, up which the MG was racing, drawing away from the heavier Cord with its two passengers, behind which Apple had come so close that he was now ready to veer out for passing.

"SLOW DOWN!" Mavis Whittington shouted, strongly jerking Apple's arm.

Both Prunella and Jacob Planter looked behind. The latter's face, in respect of Ethel's attempt at overtaking, was an amused *Are you kidding?*

One-handed, still trying to pull free of the archaeologist's grip, one brought to blacksmith potency by years of pick-and-shovel work, Apple steered out into the other lane. He looked down nervously at a lever under the dashboard.

Ethel had always had the Ribblington Overdrive. It had been built into her during her days with the Vice Squad. Apple had never used the powerful contraption. In a quiet, damp, rare-visited corner of his mind he felt Ethel was too old to be subjected to such violence.

The Ribblington's time had come, Apple decided as he interpreted as admiring the glance thrown back at him by Prunella, whose elsewise attitude showed that she believed Ethel to be outclassed.

Mavis Whittington boomed her protests, the music pounded like rapid surf, and Apple steered at wobbly speed while trying to free his arm in order to move that lever.

Leaning his head out through the window he turned it semibackwards long enough to shout, "Sorry, but I have to slow down now!"

"ABOUT TIME!"

"Let my arm go!"

"RIGHT YOU ARE!"

Freed from the grip, Apple reached under the dashboard. He fingered the lever and wondered: Should he or shouldn't he? Was it worth it?

Cynically, Jacob Planter put his arm out and began to sweep it forward: permission to pass.

Apple pushed the lever down.

At once, as though she were being towed, Ethel moved swoopingly forward.

Despite the shrill-whining grind from somewhere below, Apple was thrilled. He even had the presence of stimulated mind to roll his window up—just defeating a grab from Dr. Whittington, who buckled her hand on the glass.

Ethel roared on, gaining ground beside the Cord. Jacob Planter did tennis-judge at speed and Prunella thrilled Apple further with a gape.

At the fist racketing on his window he nodded amiably. For his own benefit he performed a short spasm of conducting to the thundering music.

Ethel drew steadily on until she was near to neck and neck with the convertible, at which juncture Mavis Whittington opened Apple's door.

She bellowed in, "I SAID—"

He snatched the door closed and snibbed its lock, which moment of inattention, of slowing, allowed Jacob Planter to edge in front.

What was unfair, Apple explained, was that, the Cord being on the other side from him, its occupants couldn't see the problems he was having with Mavis Whittington. It wouldn't be the same, would seem like an excuse, if he told them later, which of course he wouldn't dream of doing.

Ethel, shrilling and crackling, forged on along the now level road. Again she drew close to the convertible's front. Another quarter minute and she had reached it. A quarter minute after that and she was drawing ahead.

Ethel had taken the lead.

Embraced by wind and music and knocking, by bellows and wobbles and grinds, Apple held his gaze straight in front. His eyes were unblinking and round. He smiled tightly. *Ethel had taken the lead.*

It was a fine moment in which to be alive.

What laid on it an extra gloss for Apple was his realisation that he had no desire to glance around to see what defeat had done to Planter's face.

Ethel charged on.

On either side of the road its fences had sunk back, leaving weed-lush ground open to and level with the roadway. It was onto this that the MG now suddenly swung.

Apple, who had almost forgotten the little blue roadster, started at once to brake. As far as he was concerned, the race was over and had gone to the swiftest, namely Ethel. Slowing, he turned his wheel to steer onto the siding ground in pursuit of the doctor's car.

That move had already started to be done alongside him by the convertible. It reduced speed as it bounced, heading for where the MG was just coming to a racing stop beside a high clump of bushes.

Apple's reduction of speed was thorough: he went onto the ground at a creep: he wasn't about to risk hitting a rock hidden among the weeds.

Which he hadn't yet finished thinking about, meaning to add broken bottles and tree stumps, when, with an ugly crunch, the Cord came to a swerving, dust-raising halt.

With Ethel also stopped, Apple switched off radio and ignition, leapt out, evaded a weakly-clawing hand from behind and went forward at a run.

In passing the dust-bound convertible he called out

a casual, "Leave this to me." His run became composed of long, springing strides.

When he stopped by the MG he saw that it was empty.

FIVE

Apple circled the bushes. They were the first of a series, all taller than himself, clumps that dotted the fallow meadow stretching away on a downslope.

It was an excellent landscape into which a fugitive could make a getaway on foot, Apple acknowledged, and realised that even as he stood here the phony official could be running away openly though hidden from this point by bushes.

Without much hope of success and not a great deal of interest in same, Apple began walking parallel with the road while looking away across the meadow.

Although this affair, he knew, could be connected in any number of ways with caper sabotage, and with rally sabotage, he suspected the man who had taken the MG of being nothing more than a thief. To a professional—and he would certainly be that—the vintage sports car represented a nice little windfall.

Apple saw no signs of life, except a rabbit, which seemed less shaken by the abrupt meeting than Apple. After a final check behind two clumps of bushes he headed back.

Cautiously, a rallier came a token way to meet him, shoulders rounded and armed with a tyre-lever. A thin man with several pens clipped to his sweater's neckline, he asked, "Did the bastard get away?"

"Clean, I'm afraid."

"If I could get my hands on him . . ."

Apple nodded to indicate direction. "I didn't look behind that bush."

The man winced. "Oh, he wouldn't hang around. Not now he's lost Mavis's car."

"How is the MG?"

"Perfect. Not a scratch. Talk about luck."

That and the dare-devil exploits of Ethel and Agent One, Apple thought. He said, "Sure."

The man, cheerfully: "But poor old Planter. Sad to relate, he's had it."

"Had it?"

"Busted his steering on a rock. It's fixable, no tragedy, but it means a few days in dock."

Smiling inside his mouth Apple stated, "Jacob Planter is out of the rally."

"No, his fancy car is," the man said. "He says he's going to continue."

Apple did an inner wipe around with his tongue. He said, "Ah well."

"With Prunella Bank."

Blowing out his cheeks: "How jolly."

"They do seem to be getting along well together, those two," the man said. "Maybe it'll help; he's as mad as hell about that steering."

They went back to the open roadside, where all the others had arrived and were gathered in a huff of anticlimax by the Cord's front, under which, Apple saw on joining the group, Jacob Planter had eeled himself on his back.

After the thief or saboteur or prankster's intentions had been discussed and reviled, and after two or three of the ralliers had tuttingly shaken their heads at Apple for having allowed the swine to slip through his fingers, one man stepped forward with a growled:

"And I have something to say to you, Porter."

It was the owner of the Morris, last car but one in the chase. A sturdy neckless man with heavy spectacles which he continually adjusted as though they were a secret weapon, the retired politician asked, "Haven't I, Phyllis?"

"You have indeed," the woman who was slightly to his rear said. His wife and former speechwriter was sturdy also but had more neck, as well as a watch on each wrist.

Apple asked, "What's the something?"

Man: "Right."

Wife: "You're going to give him a piece of your mind for that assault back there."

"For your assault, Porter," the ex-politician said, "I am going to give you, free of charge, a piece of my mind."

His wife said, "If he thinks he can get away with it he's got another think coming."

"You've got another think coming, Porter," the man said, "another entirely, if, I say to you, and say quite plainly without fear of contradiction, without hardship or struggle, if . . . if . . ."

Wife: "He thinks he can get away with it."

"Yes. That's what you think."

Prunella, who had been watching placidly, asked, "What assault are you talking about?"

"You newcomers seem to have the notion you can commit murder," the ex-politician said. Pushing his eye-glasses up on his nose attackingly, he accused Apple, "You bashed me brutally in the back."

From the group, gasps. Some people tried to see behind the man before understanding and looking toward the Morris, whose owner said, "By a miracle, to mention nothing of my skilled handling of the car, there's no damage."

"Except to me," his wife said. She clasped the back of her neck and raised her eyebrows drastically in the middle. "He's given me whiplash."

Shuffling uncomfortably Apple offered, "Sorry. But it was an accident."

"Tommyrot and rubbish and bedpans," the man snapped. "It was quite deliberate."

"That's true," the woman said.

Apple: "No it isn't."

Man: "Yes it is. De-liberate."

Prunella asked, "Why on earth did you do that, Apple?" While he was shaking his head she added, "I didn't think you were the type."

"I'm not," Apple said. "It's not true."

The man asked, "And just what, pray, is that supposed to mean?"

His wife said, "Obviously, darling, he's calling us liars or dreamers."

From the group, indrawn breath. From Apple, who for the life of him could think of nothing devastating to use, a bored-sounding "This is stupid."

Wife: "Stupid liars or dreamers."

Her husband grated, "Are you suggesting, Porter, that my good lady and I, regular churchgoers both, property owners and taxpayers and voters, would stoop to telling pathetic lies in order to accomplish nothing whatever?"

"Not suggesting a thing."

"We do not ask for gold, Porter. We do not ask for succour. We do not ask for an eye for an eye, a tooth for a tooth. We do not ask for . . . um . . ."

"Justice," the woman said.

"No, we don't, Porter. Not at all."

Apple: "Good."

The woman said, "What we would like is an apology for his outrageous behaviour."

Prunella murmured, "Really, Apple."

Apple stood tall and rigid. "To whom it may concern," he said. "My hitting with my car the rear of the Morris was an accident, due entirely to my efforts to aid a lady in distress. I am sorry about minuscule scratches on bumpers and slight strains in necks, but—"

The voice which cut in here was so unattractive, so harsh, that Apple failed to recognise it until its owner rose into view from behind the circle of ralliers, who then gave way to Jacob Planter with eager shuffles.

The inventor had said, "Don't expect an apology from *him*." In one hand he held a wrench.

Apple: "I beg your pardon?"

"You heard what I said, Porter, and I don't expect an apology either."

Prunella asked him, "What d'you want one for, Jake?"

"For what happened here five minutes ago. The way he ran me off the road like that."

There were more gasps, which lingered when the inventor slapped the wrench into the palm of his hand in accepted threat fashion.

He said, "Go on, Porter, deny it."

Apple said, "Of course I do. It's ridiculous."

While Prunella was saying she had to say it hadn't seemed to her as though the Cord had been forced off the road, Planter loudly insisted that it was so, and Apple was finding the situation not dangerous but curious.

Although he knew that it was common for people to jump on the bandwagon, hail a hero or stone a suspect, Apple felt that Jacob Planter's accusation was too contrived and his belligerence too theatrical.

Or could it be, Apple questioned in fleet passing, that the inventor was simply showing his justifiable rage at an off-roading which actually did happen but which the culprit was denying to himself? Apple doubted it but wasn't one hundred per cent sure.

Jacob Planter started moving closer. He palm-slapped his wrench while saying he wanted satisfaction one way or another and with Apple saying that perhaps what he really wanted was a course of driving lessons.

Eyeing the wrench and its bearer's attitude of menace, people had begun making conciliatory murmurs, sounding like new-fed doves. Accidents would happen, some offered to each other with large nods. The ex-politician looked wistful and his wife looked furious.

Prunella told everyone, "This has to stop."

One man stepped in front of the inventor with a placating "Now now, old chap."

Pushing around him Jacob Planter said, "Old chap yourself." But he halted, as expected, when next Apple used a ploy from Training Five. He said:

"I don't know why you're afraid of me."

Planter came close to spluttering with his, "What're you blathering about? Afraid of you?"

"You're big enough to not need a weapon."

That took care of the wrench. After a brief hesitation Jacob Planter tossed it aside and wasn't distracted even a blink's worth when it landed on someone's foot. His right fist was the weapon he poised for use as he swiftly covered the remaining ground.

The attack was on.

To a chorus of exclamations, theme one of open

concern with a descant of hidden glee, the pair of tall men tangled. That first punch of the attacker hissed past Apple's ear. A left scraped across his ribs.

He was slow in warming up, retaliating. Things were happening too fast for him to remember the appropriate combat response to amateur attacks that happened fast.

The ex-politician shouted, "Go it, Planter." Prunella told him, "Shut bloody up."

Apple had almost remembered what to do when the uppercut landed jarringly on his chin. He went straight into a stiff backwards fall.

With his confusion beginning to evaporate Apple found himself lying on the ground. The lumpiness pressing against most of his body was rendered acceptable, even enjoyable insofar as it was useable for lordly comparison, by the comfort of his head and shoulders.

They were resting on Prunella's lap. Apple, snuggling, wondered lazily if she had called Jacob Planter a brute.

The attacker stood with folded arms. He was being patted by people as though he were a good little doggie or in congratulation for following the adage about not kicking a man when he was down.

Although he no more knew than his victim did that he represented a sneery kid, Jacob Planter's expression implied sulky pleasure at his having shown he had more to offer than just a new bike.

Apple sighed at the richness of it all. If it hadn't been for this lap and the cool hand on his brow, he vigorously assured himself, he would have leapt up with a throaty cry and turned the inventor inside out. But then, Prunella might be far from impressed. In any case, he was liable to get everything wrong, and lose.

Apple had finished getting the most out of a thorough whimper, which gratuitously brought a cozy stroking by the hand, when a female voice asked:

"More problems?"

Trundling to a stop among the twitchy spectators was Mavis Whittington. Her face was a fair colour match for her hair and she had lost the mien of command. In answer to the same question from ten people she said she had been resting in that deathtrap of a taxi.

Prunella: "Are you all right, dear?"

"I'm shattered," the doctor said. "Absolutely. Speed unravels me." She stared at Apple with tired venom. "It's all his fault."

Apple: "I was trying to rescue your car."

"And your car," Prunella said quickly, "is in the pink of condition."

Mavis Whittington said, "Wish I was."

"But isn't it good, dear, your MG being fine?"

Absently: "Very."

"The thief got away."

Same: "Very."

"I went after him alone, before the others arrived," Apple said in an invalid voice, raising a limp hand. "I did my best for you, Mave."

Four people told Dr. Whittington why Apple was on the ground and for what reason Jacob Planter had put him there. She said a weary, indifferent, "Can't say I noticed any off-roading."

Apple was distantly unnerved to find he had the urge to put out his tongue at Jacob Planter, who glared at the archaeologist, who asked plaintively, "Now who'll help me out?"

One person, edging away like the others, asked, "What kind of help's needed?"

"Somebody to take me and my car to the nearest hotel. I'm finished with driving for the next few days."

"You mean you're out of the rally?"

"I do. Car and self. Completely. The barbarity of high speed did me in."

Thought it might, Apple mused, sitting up brightly. I played it right.

There was a dizzy confusion in his head again. He realised he had made a mistake in moving so fast so soon. However, having performed the tough-guy, quick-recovery routine, Apple would not have lain down again for the gift of a pair of reverse elevator shoes.

He was normal once more by departure time. Prunella drove the doctor's car, crawling, Jacob Planter squeezed in with the ex-politician and wife.

The group got back to the other cars and their guard, who listened avidly to what had gone on while pretending to be disinterested, a feat which made Apple go prickly in the armpits with envy.

It was an hour before the motorcade got on its way, minus Cord and MG. Mavis Whittington had to be accompanied en masse to a hotel and thoroughly said farewell to once she had settled in; Jacob Planter had to be waited for while he arranged at a garage for the collection of his car.

Darkness had long since fallen when they at least arrived at the rally's overnight stop.

Too late for dinner, the group, washing but not changing, ate a cold supper at a shared table. It was surrounded by other, standing ralliers, who were keeping their annoyance hidden as they heard all

about the group's adventures and who enjoyed looking judgements at Apple.

He didn't care. Although he wasn't sitting next to
Prunella, neither was the inventor. He ignored the
mutter from someone behind of "It's these new types
who're always in trouble." With everyone standing
being in evening dress, he felt as though he were in a
high-stakes game at Monte Carlo. It wasn't such a bad
feeling.

Because of the threat of theft, the matter of
nightwatchers was revised. There would be stronger
shifts, the Council of War decided. Apple was given
the midnight-to-four, along with three other male ralliers.

"Right," he said, beginning to get up. "I'll try to fit
in a couple of hours' sleep."

The casino rubberneckers parted to let him by,
shifting with sideways movements as though he had
something that could be caught. It made him feel
dangerous.

He didn't get far across the dining room from the
grouping before someone, an official, stopped him
with, "This business between you and Planter."

"What about it?"

"It has to be settled without delay. We can't have
running feuds, y'know."

The inventor, also up from the table, was among
people and being manoeuvred this way, Apple noted
as he listened to the official go on with:

"It's all perfectly normal, y'know. Nothing the
least outlandish about it. Arguments and even fisti-
cuffs are a part of every rally. This one, in fact, has
been unusually quiet in that respect. Because, I suppose, everybody's been preoccupied with the sabotage."

There was nothing like an outside threat to draw people together, Apple remarked, and the official said that was it exactly, that was what he was getting at, quite.

Feeling wise and appreciated, Apple was malleable when Jacob Planter had been steered close. In identical wording, as if there were a set formula for this occurrence, like asking upstarts just who they thought they were anyway, several people said, "Now shake hands, you two."

The handshake was brought off with both men swaying with their heads down like convicts shuffling in a slow queue. The inventor mumbled what could have been an apology. Apple's mumbles could have been whatever an auditor wanted to make them into.

"*There* you are," people said.

Each peacemaker's smile, a statement that to its owner alone must go the credit for having produced this coup, took on condescension when meeting the smile of another, so that as Apple and Jacob Planter were leaving, urged into walking out of the dining room together, they left behind them people who were regarding one another with forgiveness and pity.

"Too bad about your car," Apple said stiffly.

The inventor said, "As a matter of fact it won't be time wasted, my Cord being in the garage."

"No? Good."

"While it's being repaired they'll give the motor a complete tune-up."

"Running a bit too fast, eh?"

"Been running badly," Planter said in subdued snaps. "Very badly. Very badly indeed."

"So has Ethel. Awful."

"Sluggish, that's the word."

"Ethel has one spark-plug missing," Apple said, and, assuring himself that his lies were all part of the caper, venial, went on to tell about Dr. Whittington inadvertently strangling him while he was trying to drive.

Jacob Planter, muttering, was unable to come up with anything other than repeats of how badly his Cord had been running. It was pathetic, Apple thought, stroking his chin. Sad.

The reception desk, as instructed, brought him awake with a telephone call at a quarter to midnight. Eighteen minutes later, still half asleep, he was outdoors among the cars on the hotel's parking area, saying to three men who were approaching out of the semidarkness, "I've been waiting for ages."

So had they, they said. It was their turn, they said, to sleep like pigs. They were on the first shift, they said.

As they were going inside, the other replacements came out. They had the sardonic sharp-eyed manner of accountants. The way they looked at Apple stated clearly that they considered him to be red-ink material.

The nightwatch started its patrol. This consisted of a slow circling and bisecting of the cars under lighting that was adequate.

Apple, who had been planning sabotage, mainly against Henry Caption's Bentley, soon saw that unless his colleagues got bored he would have to give up the idea: one or another of the trio was always in sight of him.

He was drawing close to the Bentley for the tenth time, and casually looking around, when with a shriek of his nerves he almost bumped into a hooded figure.

Which gave a squeal. The voice belonged to Prunella. She wore a heroine cloak with a hood. "You scared me," she said.

"Really?" Apple said lightly, the debonair hero. His heart was settling from that shriek.

"I came out to see how you were."

"I'm implacable."

Prunella put down her hood revealingly. "I was talking about the punch. It was powerful."

The attack, Apple's dismissing response implied, was the kind of thing he experienced a couple of times a week. When Prunella's eyes appeared to be on the verge of showing disappointment he switched to saying he could still feel the effects. "And thank you again for your help."

"Delighted," Prunella said, back to bright. "I'm really a frustrated nurse."

Apple gave a short laugh. It served both to abnegate any hurt he might be in the mood for feeling and to keep from cracking that he had never met a nurse who was.

"I'm proud of you, Apple, for not wanting to get up and fight on. These things're so juvenile."

"The whole bit was a mess."

"But at least I did get the opportunity of driving the MG. It's a little gem."

After Apple had asked how the doctor's car had been started by the failed thief (the wires had been crossed), he asked, "Shall we stroll?"

"I think it's a bit too chilly," Prunella said. "Be nice to sit in Ethel."

They made their way there covertly, which, Apple reflected, was probably the only dose of excitement he would come across tonight. The Henry Caption vehicle he would deal with sometime tomorrow, without sabotage.

It was cordial in Ethel's back after the night's cool. They say close. Prunella said, "You may put your arm around me, if you're so inclined, young man."

Apple cleared his throat during the zestful putting into encirclement of his arm. "There."

"Good. Now praise me madly."

Apple said, "You've maintained that Buick of yours in tremendous style."

"Thanks."

"And I'm not just saying that."

"Okay."

"I mean it."

Following a pause, Prunella said, softly, "Tell me things, Apple."

Lowering his voice also he said, "It'll be company, I suppose, having Jacob Planter riding with you again tomorrow."

"Actually, he won't be. This evening was enough. I asked him nicely to find a lift with someone else."

"Rather boring type, I imagine."

Prunella said, "Not at all. Fascinating man. The problem is, he keeps telling me how to drive."

"Not only is that atrocious manners," Apple said, "it's like advice from a loser." He would have gone on, derided Planter for having stupidly driven his car into the weeds, if Prunella hadn't said:

"You may hold my hand, if you wish, young man."

Doing so, Apple was able to keep his mind off a consideration of why it should be enjoyable, when holding his own hand would do nothing for him, by listening to the footfalls.

These, coming and going, had the rapidity of annoyance. With a song in his heart, Apple realised that the trio were missing their suspect colleague.

The song blossomed as Prunella said, lifting her face toward him, "You may venture a kiss, young man, if such appeals to you."

Apple, appreciating the fact that he was no slow coach, decided to kiss neither her hand nor her cheek but her lips. This he did, after moving in slowly so she wouldn't be taken by surprise.

It was a good kiss. It lingered as though lonely. The next one was even better. The third, when it finally came, was made more blistery by Apple realising that his hand, free of the hold, was sauntering its way inside the cloak.

Out there in reality the footsteps came and went, spaced by hisses that could have been curses.

Meeting no hindrance, Apple's impetuous hand sauntered on until it found a breast, which it gladly embraced. Prunella made a purring sound.

She and Apple twitched apart at the rapping. Looking around Apple saw three dim shapes peering through the window like waifs locked out of the workhouse.

"Took you long enough," he said, cunning and fast.

In their various ways the nightwatchers asked what he meant by that. He said, "We were testing you. I could've had the motor out by now."

"Having yourself a quiet little necking session, more like," one of the men said in bitterness. "While we stand guard like fools."

"Get with it, Porter," another said as they moved on.

The third man threw back, "For things like this you could get chucked out of the rally."

Disengaging herself, Prunella said, "You do seem to have a talent for making people dislike you."

Apple told her, and then wished he hadn't, "Takes years of practice." It didn't sound anywhere near as effective as when he had heard it in a movie the other week.

They got out and headed for the hotel entrance, walking hand in hand. There, Prunella asked, "Tell me, Apple, do you like bold women?"

"Well, I—"

"Never mind." She gave him a fast kiss. "Good night."

When he was alone Apple, wearing the kind of fatuous grin he would hate to be seen in, began to patrol. Quite some time passed before he returned to business, to the question of how he was going to nobble the cars of the remaining could-be border-skippers, Henry Caption and Adele Pringle.

It was a fine day. Apple acknowledged repeatedly as he drove what a fine day it was. This way he avoided the reminder that his adjective should not be "fine" but "last."

Awkwardly, Apple's position in the day's run was a little ahead of Caption's and a good way behind Pringle's. He didn't want to arouse suspicion by either a dawdler or a sprinter being, even if he had firmed his plans, which he had not, but he did acknowledge that it was certainly one very fine day.

Apple's chance came at the border with Austria. When he arrived there midmorning he found queues of cars on this side whereas usually at international borders the leaver gets waved through or dealt with briskly while the entrant is given the full treatment from Customs and Immigration.

But, as Apple knew, at crossings the unexpected was standard. To defeat smuggling, for example, officials who for a week have searched under seats will spend an evening looking nowhere but in door-pockets.

In this case, Apple listed, the cause of delay could range from a staff shortage, pigheadedness or sloth to an alert for the prevention of escape from the country of a national treasure/a criminal/stolen goods.

It was on seeing a 1929 Flying Standard close to the front of the queue that Apple, still partly in his dwell on Customs, got his idea. He gave it a smiling welcome and quickly steered out of line.

He went only a short distance, to a pair of telephones. Of the cowl type, one was occupied and the other, for use by the wheelchair-bound, was available.

If Adele Pringle had been farther back in the queue, Apple assured himself, he would most certainly have waited until the regular telephone was free. It was shortage of time that took him to the other, beside the low-set equipment at which he squatted instead of bending, which would have given him lumber pain.

To get the right number took four calls. The Standard drew ever closer to the front and Apple's agitation wasn't helped by the caller beside him.

The sturdy matron with a Berlin accent, having had her turn at overtalk to Klaus, had started to be his listener. In being so she no longer gazed at nothing but looked down at Apple.

She despised him. Her eyes said he was an animal. He was a mocker of invalids. He was an abuser of hard-won privileges. At one point she stopped her silence long enough to tell Klaus she wished he could just see this.

With underneath his agitation a masochistic tingle born of his being consistent in his attracting of odium, closet son of a bitch that he might be, Apple made the final connexion. A voice clicking with busyness identified itself as belonging to a border official.

"This is headquarters," Apple said in military German. "Is that Schmidt?"

Busyness gone: "There's no Schmidt here, sir. I'm Wankel."

Following a grumble that he couldn't keep up with all these changes nowadays, Apple went on, "We've had an anonymous telephone call. It relates to an English car with United Kingdom plates, a Standard."

"Licence number, sir?"

Automatically, although knowing the licence plate would be unseeable, Apple craned a look around his despiser, who watched on though she couldn't hear what he was saying in respect of content.

Apple's crane caused the woman to draw air in loudly through her nose. The act was so offensive in its accusation of all manner of corruptions, including theft from the blind, that Apple craned again.

Into the mouthpiece he said, voice low, "Number unknown. But the colour is brown and the model is a 1929."

"Wait," the man said. "Wait a minute." He sounded excited. "There's an old brown car coming level with the window now."

Doing a good crane, Apple saw the Standard's roof at the queue front. "That could be the one, Wankel," he said. In leaning back he glanced up sly-eyed at the woman, who at once showed the gums above her top teeth.

"Is it in a rally, sir?"

"That's the one," Apple said. "A British group.

The driver of the car is completely innocent. Her name is Pringle. She's fortyish, stout, square of face and has her hair cut like one of our dear old helmets."

"Yes, this is the right car."

"She's a famous poet, has Prussian blood in her veins and must be treated with velvet gloves."

"Leave it to me, sir," the official said. "I'm used to these delicate situations."

"Good man, Wankel."

"And what is the problem with the car, sir?"

Unaware of flicking his eyes upward and of raising his voice, Apple said, "Opium." After hearing an appreciative response from the official and seeing from the women one of tension he added, "I must have it."

"Yes, sir."

"I must, I must."

"Naturally, sir."

Voice down again Apple explained that as the narcotic had been smuggled into this country in the car, unbeknownst to Ms. Pringle, scorn would be poured on the efficiency of German Customs and Excise if it was discovered by the Austrians, as it was bound to be if not located on this side of the border, for they had a new dog over there, a brilliant Pekingese sniffer.

"I didn't know that, sir."

"It's just arrived," Apple whispered, noting the woman's steep lean above him. "We don't know where the hiding place is but that's your department."

"Don't worry about that, sir."

With a hand to his brow Apple again raised his voice for "I must have that opium."

"We've never failed yet, sir."

After saying in a mutter that he would be in touch,

and stressing that in the official's hands lay the reputation of the service, and pretending not to hear him
when he asked for the caller's name, Apple disconnected.

He rose to his feet without giving in to the urge to
whimper. However, to make himself taller he took to
his toes, even though he couldn't see much reason in
it personally.

The woman withered back behind more showing
of upper gums in a hypocrite smile. She began hissing into the receiver the moment the addict was back
inside his car.

Whistling at how well he had brought off his original idea of an anonymous telephone call and at how
good of him it was to have shared with another person some of the caper's drama, Apple drove around
and joined on the end of the queue. The Flying Standard was nowhere to be seen.

In spurts, the queue moved ahead. As soon as he
got over into Austria, Apple mused, he would embark
on the derailing of Henry Caption.

It was when Ethel had come to within three or
four cars of the front that a rallier came panting up to
her. The man said, "Thank God."

Apple, warily: "Eh?"

"It's Adele Pringle. She's having an awful time
with the Customs people."

"Ah well."

"The problem is language," the man said. "So if
you'll just come with me, please."

Although Apple opened his mouth for a protest,
none came out. To refuse to assist the poet would not
only be atrocious but pointless, as he knew that if he
drove on he would sooner or later have to turn
around and come back, quickly, avoiding jabs from

the pitchfork of a conscience with no conscience of its own.

After parking out of the line Apple followed to a door in the red-brick building, where the rallier said, "In there. Now I really must be getting along." He looked at Apple accusingly. "This has caused me a lot of delay."

"Sorry about that."

"So long, Porter."

Apple entered the building briskly. This business he would have over and done with, he promised himself, before you could say Jack, son of Robin.

The two hours of frustration that followed would have been difficult for Apple even without Adele Pringle's cigarettes. He coughed as much as she did but less than the two officials who spent that time delving into the Standard's every cranny and item of luggage.

The men also wanted to know all the poet's movements prior to her arrival in Germany, in hopes of elbowing her memory into producing the individual who had sneaked narcotics into her car or the place where it might have happened. Tamely and glumly, Apple translated.

It was not until the officials said they would now start on the tyres and inner tubes, and if that failed would have to send to Berlin for an expert, that Apple rebelled.

"Sorry," he said. "I can't wait any longer."

"I've had it too," Adele Pringle said. "This could take till tomorrow. And fruitlessly. I'll bet anything there's no dope hidden in Roderick."

"You could be right, Pring." They had been through this exchange a dozen times.

"It's more sabotage, probably, along the lines of your chicken-killing. What a swinish trick."

Looking down: "True."

"Ask them, please, if I'm free to go."

He asked. Coughing, the men said that would be perfectly all right, yes, fine.

"Righto," Adele Pringle said, turning to Apple. "I'll finish the rally with you."

His eyes were red, his throat hurt and his lungs felt as though they were competing one with the other for grittiness. During the past hour cigarette smoke had been billowing in at him through the open glass panel, beyond which sat Adele Pringle on the folding seat.

It was such a nice change to have someone to chat with on the journey, she had said, and would he mind awfully keeping his window rolled securely up, she didn't want to get pleurisy a second time.

Ignoring the obtuse consideration that this—physical discomfort, delay, being thwarted planwise—was some manner of retribution for landing the innocent in trouble, Apple again gave his mind to the question of his passenger. How was he going to get rid of her?

As all along, however, cogitation for Apple was made toilsome by talk. What he had read somewhere seemed to be true, he saw, that while novelists were cheap with words in speech due to spending them lavishly in writing, poets were the reverse. Adele Pringle's tongue was rarely still.

But, savingly, one small grace, her talk was impersonal, light and eclectic. Never once did she mention that her beloved Roderick had been sequestered, which, Apple had to allow, was true blue of her.

He was dwelling lyingly on the scheme of knocking Adele out with a rock, the while listening to a description of her last poetry reading, when he steered around a bend in the country road and came in sight of a tavern.

The place itself was of no interest to him; in order to make up for squandered time he had declined to stop for lunch and had no intentions of stopping now; he could manage on the black bread and cheese supplied by coughing Customs.

What gave Apple large pause was seeing, among other parked vehicles, several of them belonging to BOVA members, a 1935 Bentley. Immediately he began to drive slowly and think at speed. His mind scrambled for an idea.

Cheerfully Adele Pringle asked, "Oh, are we going to stop after all?"

Apple said, "My God."

"What is it?"

"Well, I'll be a donkey's uncle."

"What's wrong, Apple?"

He turned onto the edge of the dirt parking area. "Would you believe it."

Adele said, "I can't stand suspense."

"It's the craziest thing."

"I've been known to scream."

The scrambled-for idea finally came as he brought Ethel to a halt. The relief made him sag, which droop he pretended was due to dejection.

He said. "It's no good, I'll have to go back. And be quick about it."

Adele: "Back to the border, you mean?"

Apple nodded like a horse. While opening the door and getting out, now acting agitation but gratefully taking deep draughts of clean air, he explained that if he didn't go back it could die.

"What could?"

"The goldfish. I bought it this morning. Nice little thing. I took her bowl out of the car while I was waiting in that slow queue, to give her a bit of an outing."

The better to look at him, it appeared, Adele Pringle opened the rear door. "It's nice," she said in a dull voice, "a change."

"I put the bowl down and forgot all about it," Apple said. He was pleased with his decency in not putting the blame on having to do Adele's translating, though beneath that he knew that said blame was the correct way to handle the situation: make them amenable by feeling at fault.

Adele said, "I see."

"I'm quite upset, as a matter of fact."

"Yes, your eyes are red."

Apple was tempted to embroider, tell of the attachments he had formed in his life with various goldfish. But he felt the urgency. There was no knowing how long Henry Caption would be here.

"So I'll leave you off to cadge a ride with one of the other ralliers," Apple said. "I wouldn't dream of dragging you back with me."

"Oh, I don't mind."

"No no. If we broke down you might miss the rally's last night, the gala dinner and everything. The fun. The music. The performance of Enrico Balto."

"Won't kill me."

"The poetry reading you're going to give."

Pulling on a suitcase, Adele Pringle began to alight. She said, "Well, thank you for . . ."

Two minutes later Ethel was speeding back along the road. That, the speed, lasted only until the tavern was no longer to be seen. Apple started carefully examining the roadsides for a place of concealment.

He grew jittery, one leg dithering. Not the least of his problems, he recognised, was that if the useable place were too far away it would take him forever to get back, even if he went by the road, which was out of the question.

A gate appeared.

On the left, it stood slightly ajar. There were still no other cars around. Even while accepting the opportunity Apple fretted that it should be so perfect.

At a spin of the steering-wheel Ethel made the turn and stopped with the gate six inches away. Apple eased her forward. Metal touched wood and wood began to ease back, wailing.

With the gate neatly scuffed back Apple drove through. A pair of wheel-tracks led him around the tip of a long stretch of woodland, from where the road was out of sight. Ethel locked, he set off back to the tavern over fields.

He ran easily. His mind he kept off what lay ahead. In respect of yesterminute he refused even to acknowledge how vapid it would be if he were to feel uncomfortable about leaving a stupid gate open.

Soon approaching the tavern, where still stood the ex-athlete's car, Apple stopped to dodge into hiding as a couple came out. They were BOVA. When they had driven off he went on again, making straight for the Bentley.

This was a tricky bit, Apple's stomach announced. Henry Caption could come out at any second. If he did, if he saw Appleton Porter getting into or driving away his car, it would surely spell the last word of Porter's connexion with the rally, and the rally was the caper.

The door-lock gave no trouble. It responded like an instructor's model to the skeleton-key. Apple slipped inside behind the wheel. From a corner of his vision he saw a figure come out of the tavern.

That it wasn't the Bentley's owner was all he established as he threw himself down on the seat, from which position, conveniently, worryingly, he was able to sort out wires under the dashboard. He had the right pair isolated by the time he heard a car leaving.

Sitting up cautious as a mother bird Apple dealt with the two wires. He started the motor, engaged gear, released the handbrake, moved forward. No one appeared.

Not until he was leaving dirt for hardtop did Apple realise that where he had left Ethel would do as well as anywhere as stashing place.

Although not in love with the idea of a long hike, Apple had thought of taking the Bentley far, far away. But he agreed now with his lazy side, who said distance wasn't the point and that the best place of all would be in a shed right at the tavern's rear.

In heading swiftly for the gateway Apple made a reminder that tomorrow he would telephone the police anonymously to let them know where the stolen car could be found. Since anonymous calls didn't always work out as expected, he thought this plan pretty benevolent of him, which balanced a counterthought in respect of theft from an innocent party.

Arriving without incident back at Ethel, Apple uncoupled the ignition wires, for the hell of it attended to fingerprints, got out and locked the door. At a creep he went to the gate, which he closed and then returned to a minute later in order to stand ajar, leave

the way he had found it. He told himself a good operative always saw to details like that.

With at least an hour to put behind him Apple began to stroll, circling within sight of the two cars.
There was flora, pale sunshine, birdsong. There was
clean air.

This can't be bad, Apple thought.

Time passed. As it did, Apple covered more
ground than he would have in the hike he had
avoided, but that being a need and this a gift, he
didn't feel tired.

Judging the time-lapse as right, Apple left. Gate
stood as before, he headed for the tavern, on whose
parking area a solitary rally car was being entered by
its owner. From the woman Apple learned facts:

Henry Caption's Bentley had been stolen. The police had been and gone. Adele Pringle had found a
ride with someone.

"And who did Caption get a ride with?"

"No one," the woman said. "He quit the rally."
She pressed her starter. "How's the goldfish?"

Even while feeling a chill down their spines most
motorists scoff when they hear the rhythmic bumping that sounds like a tyre going flat, sure it means
something else or trying to will it to be.

Apple belonged to that school, a teacher. Now he
went so far as to laugh aloud at the bumping because
of how ridiculously inappropriate it would be for
him to have a puncture. He needed one like he
needed more freckles.

Ethel started to shake to the bumps and her every
window set up a chatter. His laugh gone, Apple came
to a fast stop on the road's narrow shoulder.

At least it did have a shoulder of sorts, he consoled

unhappily on getting out, just as he had the luck for this to have happened here where the traffic was light and not on a major highway, where transport monsters hurtled past like tracer bullets.

Even so, when Apple at length had the offside rear corner shakily jacked up on sandy ground, every vehicle that did go by made Ethel rock like a tipsy tart in the backlash of wind.

Apple mused that what was really annoying him was not the toil and bother but the fact that this would cancel out the excellent time he had been making. He had passed eight or ten other rally cars.

They now began to do the passing. It came as no surprise to the toiler that nobody stopped to offer assistance. Those who didn't smile, waved.

Apple had the culprit wheel off when one of the ralliers did come to a dawdle alongside him. He called out, "She's not badly hurt."

"I know," Apple said. "It's a puncture."

"No, it was an accident."

"I didn't suggest it was sabotage."

"I didn't either."

Apple stared. He then joined the man in asking, "What're you talking about?"

The car was creeping on. Its driver said, "Prunella Bank. A lady you know rather well, I hear."

"What about her?"

"She had an accident."

Apple let the wheel fall and straightened. "Prunella had an accident?"

"On a stretch of main highway, a good drive ahead of here. I got the word on my CB radio."

Because people hearing bad news often try to change the subject, especially to the frivolous, Apple said, "Two-way radios are against the rules."

"You going to report me?"

"An accident, did you say?"

The man said, "I did."

Walking along beside the still-moving car Apple asked snappingly for the hows, whys and whens. He grabbed the windowsill: "It wouldn't kill you to stop for a minute."

Car stopped, its driver said he knew very little. "One of those juggernauts with a trailer passed her and cut into the inside lane too sharply. The trailer whipped over and slapped the front of her. She ran off the road."

"And she's not hurt?"

"A big scrape and a buckled wheel."

"I'm talking about Ms. Bank."

"Oh, just knocked about a bit," the man said. "She seems to have survived." He revved his engine impatiently. "The truck didn't stop but a passing motorist took her to the nearest first-aid place, wherever that might be."

"So where's the accident?"

"You'll see it as you go by. The Buick won't have been towed away yet. It's out of the rally, of course."

"That's a shame."

"But my Essex isn't," the man said. "So long." The car slipped away.

Sharing his fume between the rallier's casual attitude, Ethel's punctured tyre and the bullying hit-and-run truck driver, Apple bustled like a mechanic on piecework to get the job finished.

His thoughts he cruelly flogged away from Prunella, since he knew without a doubt that otherwise he would quickly have her prone on an operating table and with the head surgeon of the ten-man team defeatedly shaking his head; to start things off with.

Spare wheel on and firm, Apple was proud of himself for committing the solecism of pushing Ethel off the jack rather than letting it down.

He drove off.

Half an hour later, on a major traffic artery, Apple came within view of the Buick Special. Alone and forlorn, it stood at the bottom of a shallow shoulder, its front bearing a gruesome scar of silver freshness.

Enquiring at the nearest house Apple learned where, in all probability, Prunella would have been taken for medical attention. He was there inside ten minutes, a cottage hospital on a town's outskirts.

As Apple alighted from Ethel, a woman who was coming out of the building waved at him. She wore a shapeless blue dress, her head was covered by a scarf and her face was all but hidden by large wads of gauze held on with surgical tape. Also she had on a pair of sunglasses.

She said, hoarsely, "Hello. It's me."

"Good God," Apple said. He hurried over to her. "I was told you weren't badly hurt."

"I'm not. I've got this one piffling little cut, which bled like a tap."

"Head wounds bleed the most."

Prunella said, "But I've plenty of bruises and swellings here and there."

"They must be severe."

"Not at all. The ones on my face do, however, tend to detract from my fabulous beauty, and I'd rather be hidden than be seen ugly."

"You seem in good spirits, granted," Apple said. He was having the customary problem of adjusting to mundane relief from exciting dread and trying contiguously not to feel disappointed in the survivor for having let him down.

"My spirits are lovely, Apple."

Almost an accusation: "Your voice is odd."

"Thank you for noticing," Prunella said, giving one small clap. "I think it's coming along nicely."

"Translation, please."

"The voice adds something to the overall picture, don't you agree? I just have to make the most of this. I've never been involved in a traffic accident before."

Feeling drear, a wet blanket, Apple asked, "Did you get the truck's licence number?"

"Certainly not," Prunella said. "But back to me. How d'you like my poignant dress? The nurses loaned it to me. My other clothes're bloody."

"The doctor say you're okay to leave?"

"Oh yes. I've arranged with a garage for the Buick and I was about to call a taxi when you came."

"At your service," Apple said.

"All we have to do is stop briefly at the car to pick up my stuff."

"So you're continuing?"

"Intrepid, that's me," Prunella said hoarsely. "Anyway, I wouldn't miss this last night for worlds. It should be fun."

"Yes," Apple said. "It should."

SIX

The inn was one of those quasi-Alpine affairs which were put up in their thousands in the postwar reconstruction era, as though out of a need to return Austria to its familiar image of picturesque simplicity.

After a thirty years' war against weather, plus having the parking area hidden behind and television antennae out of sight among chimneys, the inn looked almost as ancient as the lonely countryside it sat in.

The lobby was equally convincing. It had rich wooden panelling galore, a minstrel gallery, an archway into the bar, glass doors leading to the dining room. A staircase of unpainted pine descended as grandly as any scion of the House of Hapsburg.

Apple couldn't help but feel vaguely regal when, in his dinner jacket, he slowly came down toward the assembly, which sparkled like a ball at the palace.

What made Apple feel all the better was that he had no right to feel that way, to be anything but despondent, since he still had no particular ideas on how to contain the three remaining Possibles: Adele Pringle, Enrico Balto and Jacob Planter, who were all present below in the lobby. Wearing their finery, each standing alone, they looked unrelaxed, like actors with first-night nerves.

Apple felt sure he would rise to the occasion ploywise, however, when the time came, which meant after nightfall. Not one move would Defector make until he had help from the dark. Even then he would have to steal a car or send to somewhere for a taxi.

There you are, Apple nudged himself in leaving the bottom step, I told you so. Bright ideas were starting already. Two, in fact. You couldn't keep a good spy down.

Leisurely Apple moved through the throng, heading for the reception desk. Once he was stopped to be told too bad about the goldfish, twice to be asked about Prunella. The fourth stop was of his own making.

"It's not all over yet, of course," he said out of the corner of his mouth.

"What isn't?"

"The danger. Theft. Sabotage. What have you. It's a good thing they're keeping up the watch on the cars."

"As mine isn't here," Jacob Planter said. "I couldn't care less." His bow-tie drooped at the same angle as his moustache, which annoyed Apple, it was so effective.

He said, "I couldn't either."

"But your car is here."

"Listen. I'm not worried about Ethel. She's up to the ears in protection and antithief devices. A thief would soon wish he hadn't bothered."

"Frankly," Jacob Planter said, drawling, "I don't know why anyone would want to bother with a commercial vehicle in the first place."

Heavily not hearing that, Apple said, "We'll have a full moon out there later, Jake. It'll be a perfect night to make a run for it."

"Run for what?"

"If it weren't for the manoeuvres being arranged by the Austrian army, I've heard."

Jacob Planter looked at him from a profile angle. "Have you been drinking?"

Still deaf, Apple said, "But I must go on my inimitable way. Take care." He went off.

After another goldfish-condolence halt, Apple reached the reception desk. While waiting for attention he reflected that although the manoeuvres lowdown wasn't so hot it did at least keep the chain of ideas going.

Next, rubbing his nose, Apple admitted that the lowdown had been not so much unhot as plain chill; a heavy-handed and greenhornish blunder in the gloom rather than a step in the right direction. He resolved from now on to leave ideas like that unsaid. There was the future to think about.

Apple owned a secret expectation, a rarely recognised belief that someday, on a misty time in the years far ahead, his career was an espionage operative would be written about and published. During sunny moments, his secret peeping out, he was wont to mull cozily over smart gambits and flattering actions. In black moments he suspected that the book would be only ten pages long.

When his turn came at the desk Apple asked what the situation was locally with taxicabs and hire cars. They could be arranged for by telephone, from Aspern, fifteen kilometres away, the manager said.

He, a man of early middle-age, suited the lobby as would a yodel, despite the sober dress in place of lederhosen. He was blond, pink and a beamer. Also he had a fat belly and lavish sideburns, was given to patting the one and stroking the others, as though they were assurances of his skill at being the jolly, helpful innkeeper.

"My car is a London taxi," Apple told him. "You may have noticed it."

"I haf, sir. Beautiful."

Switching to German with a Viennese accent: "Actually, I'm licenced to ply for hire in this country. I have dual nationality."

In the same language: "That's fascinating, sir."

"I'd only do it for fun while I'm here, and only for one of my rally colleagues. But I'd charge plenty and, of course, I'd split my fee with the management."

"Yes, most fascinating."

"Therefore if anyone enquires about hiring a car, let me know, mm, before you go any further?"

He would indeed, the manager said happily with two pats and a stroke.

People were starting to drift into the dining room as Apple strolled around the assembly's edge, hands clasped behind. He still felt regal. He came close to wondering if that future book would have photographs.

With the crowd thinning even more Apple stopped beside Adele Pringle. The poet had her inevitable cigarette stuck in an exotic holder, gold to match her evening dress and her passion for yellow.

She asked, after they had exchanged compliments on their elegance, "I don't suppose you had time to ask the Customs boys if they'd given up on Roderick, had you?"

"I had, as a matter of fact," Apple said. "That's what I came to tell you."

Perking: "And?"

"They hadn't."

"Bloody idiots," Adele Pringle rumbled. "Didn't

they even give an indication as to when I could have him back?"

"Sorry, but I didn't press the matter. I was too upset about Lucinda."

"Wasn't that awful? I don't know why anybody would want to steal a goldfish."

"Nor me," Apple said. "Unless because it's easy. Now if it were possible to have on a fishbowl all the antitheft devices I have on Ethel."

He had finished lying about that and had started talking of the dense pea-souper fog that was forecast for tonight, when Adele Pringle interrupted with:

"Look who hasn't changed."

Coming down the staircase slowly was Prunella, dressed and bandaged as before, in addition to still wearing the sunglasses, which ensemble Apple had expected. Prunella had told him, "I wouldn't dream of missing all the delicious sympathy. I might even limp."

Adele Pringle said, "Poor girl. She's probably too black and blue to get out of that dress."

"She's very brave," Apple said. "Excuse me." He moved on, his aim the staircase. That he changed on noting Enrico Balto ambling in the other direction. Apple stopped. When he saw that the singer was headed not for the exit but the bar arch, he relaxed. He followed and caught up.

"I might patent my ideas."

Balto looked at him dismally before averting his eyes. "On what?" At the end of the recital on antitheft devices he said, "But your car has been stolen. Remember?"

"Ah yes. That was because I didn't think I needed to switch the gadgets on. They're on now."

"Wonderful," Balto said as if to the dentist's news that they all had to come out. "Excuse me."

Apple detained him with "In any case, the roads could well be impassable in a while."

"That rumour about the army doing a mock attack on the hotel has been proven false."

"It isn't that," Apple said, not without a flush of author's pride. "And it's not fog, either." That, he had decided, was another chill notion.

"What is it then?"

"They say the Danube is rising."

"In that case, Porter," Enrico Balto told the arch, "you might be able to catch yourself another little fish. Excuse me." He sailed on into the bar.

Swinging around, Apple found himself facing Dr. Mavis Whittington.

She wore black velvet from large chin to ankles and wrists. Standing up aloofly from the rabble of her white hair was a tiara, which, on a closer peer, turned out to be a curved shard of ancient pottery.

"In the end I couldn't resist coming, young Appleton," she said with a hint of apology. "It is the final night, after all. The big one."

"That's true."

"And my room was booked, ready for me."

"There is that, certainly."

The archaeologist twitched herself. "You don't look madly pleased to see me here."

"Oh, but I am, I am," Apple said with one of those quick untidy nod-bows, the arms aflop. "I'm surprised and awed, that's all. It's courageous of you."

Smiling at last: "Thank you."

"Come by train?"

"No, I drove. I drove v-e-r-y slowly."

Apple gave a dull nod with the statement, "So your MG's present."

"And correct," Mavis Whittington said. She came a step nearer, her head going back. "I want to thank you for valiantly trying to help with my car. I also want to advise you to have your ears tested. It's so important, the hearing."

When the short lecture on auditory health was over Apple said, "Your car doesn't lock, does it? The thing is, there might be thieves about."

"No, but I bought one of those shriek whatsits today. If anybody tried to drive away it'd bring the house down. Don't tell anyone."

"And don't you tell anyone about Ethel. She has a dozen of those gadgets spread around her."

"Then we're both safe," Dr. Whittington said. "Excellent. Now, young Appleton, how about taking me in to dinner?"

Apple played stricken, putting on one of those toothache expressions of the socially inept. "I'd love to but I must go to my room, listen to my radio and see what's new on the threat."

"Which threat is that?"

Apple explained about the neo-Nazi group who might be going to terrorise the locality, setting fire to farms, dragging people out of their cars and shooting them, blowing up bridges. "We could be in for a state of siege."

Happily, Mavis Whittington said, "Oh, I'm so glad I came."

Apple got away.

Up in his room, which had no radio, he took from his jeans pocket a slip of paper. On it was a telephone number. Memorising it for practice he went back down to the lobby, where there were no Possibles among the stragglers.

The telephone box was under the stairs. Apple went into it, called the number and spoke urgently, disconnected and began to search through the directory for other numbers.

He had made four calls and was about to dial again when he saw Enrico come out of the bar. Following a gaze around, as though for an entourage, he set off toward the glass doors of the dining room. Apple slipped out of the box and caught up, stopping the singer with "Listen."

"I know. You might patent your ideas."

"No no," Apple said, sternly efficient. "This is another matter. Of enormous consequence to you."

"To me?" the singer asked, hand on heart.

"To Enrico Balto, the great tenor."

Smiling: "Yes?"

"Yes. So hold yourself available. Stay where I can find you without difficulty."

"Yes?"

"I'm trying to get through now. Terrible line. But even at the best of times it's not easy to contact La Scala."

Enrico Balto leaned toward Apple sideways as he rose on the toes of one foot. Looking off he began, "Did I hear you say . . . ?"

"Please don't go too far away," Apple said. He darted off and didn't look back until he was in the telephone box again and his look could be hidden by the hand-set.

Enrico Balto stood staring over from beside the glass doors, a hand still pampering his chest. He turned, but looked over once more after he had passed into the dining room.

Apple dialled. A voice answering, he went through the same routine as before, speaking German as before, in order to get connected with the news desk.

"I'll call again later to discuss terms," he said. "Let's give me the code-name of Six-Seven. Agreed?"

"If you say so."

Apple went on to tell of how Dr. Mavis Whittington, the celebrated archaeologist, was about to make a history-changing statement, a result of her recent excavations. After giving location he ended:

"Don't be put off by the lady's attitude. If she seems somewhat less than cooperative it's because she has a deal of exclusivity with an English newspaper on this sensational new development."

Apple made two more like calls before running out of useable numbers. He left the box. As he did he saw, coming toward him across the near-empty lobby, the rally official who had been his chauffeur, the little man with an underachiever goatee. His dress suit was too big for him and he swaggered as though pretending he didn't care deeply about his suspicion that people thought it borrowed.

He halted in front of Apple with a swing of loose material. Not saluting, though one arm jerked out at the elbow, he said, "No use spoiling the ship for a ha'porth of tar."

"I couldn't agree more."

"We're organised, if a little short-handed."

"I don't know what to say," Apple said honestly.

"We're guarding the cars," the official said. "Some of us are forgoing the full dinner so as to keep a lookout for the untoward. Some of us put service to the community first. Some of us are willing to risk danger."

"I think that's very fine of some of you."

"And we want you to join us, Porter. That's the best way to dispel doubts."

"Doubts about what?"

"Never mind that now. I take it you're ready and willing to start at once?"

Apple, already moving away, said, "Sorry, old man. It's impossible. If I don't eat, I collapse. Goodbye."

Wishing he could have been more inventive, come up with a snappy line, Apple went toward the dining room. Beyond its glass doors, at a far table, he noted Jacob Planter.

The connexion with what he wished he could have just been gave Apple an idea. He stopped, saw that the official was going outside, strode back to the telephone box. Inside, he found he had no change left.

At the desk Apple again had to wait, breathing deeply through his nose, until the manager had finished his beaming doings with a patron; and petulantly declined to allow that the pause let him get the story straight.

What he did reflect was how shrewd of him it had been back there not to come up with a snappy line. Had he done so he wouldn't have had that phony wish, wouldn't have made a connexion, wouldn't have got the latest idea. Sometimes it paid to keep a brake on his trenchant wit.

Jingling coins in his cupped hands Apple went back to the telephone. For this call, to police headquarters in Vienna, he used a Finnish accent in his German. What he told about Jacob Planter he did with spiteful glee, as would a rival inventor bent on mischief.

"My name is neither here nor there," he said when

the man asked for it. "Just make sure you've got my information right."

"The Englishman, an industrial spy while abroad, is prying into a project that is vital to our country."

"And there's no time to lose."

Disconnecting, Apple left the telephone box with a sly smile. It lasted until he got into the dining room, which had the noise and atmosphere of celebration. Sitting in evening dress at the nearest table was Henry Caption.

"I couldn't resist," the ex-runner said as Apple stopped at his side. "After all, it is the gala night."

"Also your room was booked."

"Exactly."

"So you hired a car."

"Not in the least. Hire cars are beyond my pocket."

"Plane, train or bus?"

"I got myself changed for dinner and started hitching rides," Henry Caption said. "Did you ever hitchhike in a dinner jacket?"

Reluctantly, Apple said, "Well, no."

"Thought maybe you hadn't."

Apple felt even more remiss when others at the table told Caption what a crazy character he was to be sure. They looked at the table-hopper coldly when he resorted to the unromantic, telling, apropos of nothing, about the antitheft devices on his car. They ignored his altogether, their talk blossoming, during his rambling discourse on the Austrian Army, fog, the rising Danube and neo-Nazis.

Apple left stiffly. Not until he was nearly there at Prunella's table did he notice that it had no vacant places. Her powerlessness to save him a seat was conveyed to him by Prunella with nifty pantomime.

Adding a false smile to his pseudo-understanding nod, Apple changed course. He searched for a place, hurt. Those available either had their backs to the room or were behind pillars. Apple looked at them with reproach.

He found a seat. It was at a table made up of three social outcasts, rich men who had been everywhere, done everything, met everyone, could talk on any topic and, if that weren't depressing enough, had started out in life with nothing. Their most-used phrase was the truism, "Yes, I know."

Being given an enthusiastic welcome mollified Apple in respect of Henry Caption turning up, Prunella not saving him a place and the dinner's first course being over. He contrived to deny that his welcome here stemmed from his taking the part of victim, that he could be a lice-ridden child-molester with an arcane disease so long as his hearing was sound.

Willing to be fair, Apple shared his attention equally among the men, who each talked at him while disregarding the others. That attention he further split:

In listening to man A, Apple flicked watchful glances to Caption, Dr. Whittington, Balto, Adele Pringle and Planter, happy diners all, it seemed; in attending to man B, he ate his fish; in playing audience for man C, he toyed with ideas for the elimination of Henry Caption.

After the third course had been cleared away there were tinklings of spoons on glasses, speeches to which only the people at that table listened, loud universal jabber during the presentation to a palpitating winner of his cup and a tomb silence while he failed to remember his impromptu speech.

The meal continued.

It was when the chicken had been served that Apple saw the men appear at the glass doors, looking in. One of them he recognised. It was the reporter he had called first tonight, the one to whom he had promised a scoop in order to get him silently away from the opera singer.

Apple's reason for sinking low over his plate he viewed as a need to keep himself out of this. It had nothing to do with promises which weren't only false but not even individual, so that the promised became merely one of the mob rather than be allowed the distinction of feeling personally abused.

His hatbrim sagging, the reporter glared about the room. This Apple saw from around the head of man A, who was talking of his last dinner at 10 Downing Street.

Switching angles, Apple looked at Enrico Balto from over the shoulder of man B, who was telling him the best days of the week for parachuting off the Eiffel Tower and not acknowledging Apple's repeated interjection that it was nine hundred and eighty-four feet tall.

Balto, having seen the reporters, having obviously assumed himself to be the sought, was preening with that pose of boredom which the would-be famous copy from the truly so, to whom it's a pose only when their fame is on the wane.

At the doors the manager appeared. Beamless, bristling discreetly, he hustled the pressmen away. Following a pause he returned, came in and went to the table of Dr. Whittington, with whom he spoke.

This, until he realised he no longer need crouch, Apple watched past man C, who was telling him about the advice he had given to the Shah of Iran.

The manager left the dining room. So did Mavis

Whittington, after she had waved away desert but finished a glass of wine. She looked puzzled and intrigued, which, Apple reckoned, meant she didn't know yet the reason for the press interest.

Time passed.

The jollification went on, dusk crept onto the windows, Dr. Mavis Whittington failed to reappear, someone went to an upright piano and knocked out a tune, Apple grew tense, his table companions told him about a garden party at Buckingham Palace, sledding down the Pyramids, a drinking session with Fats Waller.

Several voices were raised on a single theme. It was that the time had come for Adele Pringle to read her work. As the theme continued to be played by additional voices the poet fussed about herself with every indication of surprise and Enrico Balto got quietly up.

In heading for the exit the singer looked over to Apple as though on the cheery muse: Is there a connexion between the press and La Scala?

Or so Apple hoped as he got up also, rather than read the look as meaning: Is that tall character going to try to stop me going across the border?

The three men were still talking, aspiring to lure Apple back into his chair. He moved away after an encouraging nod for one, a wink of conspiracy for another and for the third an impressed tut.

In a stoop Apple began to circle toward the glass doors. As well as wearing a frown of regret he glanced frequently at his watch, man with unbreakable date, in case people were tempted to think him an ill-mannered poetry-hating lout. At the last table he stopped. He squatted beside Henry Caption.

In an undertone through firm lips he said, "Listen,

old man. There's something important I have to see
you about."

"To do with my Bentley?"

"Nothing like that. I can't go into it here. Could
you meet me later? In say twenty minutes?"

The ex-athlete said sourly, "Well, I don't know. I
don't want to miss anything."

"It'll take only a few minutes of your time."

Resigned: "Tell me where we meet."

Apple said, "There's a little writing room on the
far side of the lobby." He got up. "I'll be there in
twenty minutes. I knew I could count on you." He
moved on.

Apart from a nonrallier reading a newspaper, Enrico Balto had the lobby to himself. He stood in its
centre, shoulders back, in his bearing as he gazed
around an excess of the usual majestic to counter his
expression of bewilderment.

"The press . . . ," he began when approached by
Apple, who told him, "I won't let 'em bother you."

"Bother me?"

"La Scala might not like it."

"Yes," Enrico Balto said to the minstrel gallery,
"what's this all about."

"I'm glad you brought that up."

"One does feel an explanation is in order."

"Come on, let's go in the bar," Apple said. "I'll buy
you a drink and set things straight. I have to call Italy
again in a minute."

He strode toward the arch, forcing the singer to
follow if he wanted to be heard in his questioning.
Apple heard but didn't answer. Answers he was going to be short of. On glancing back with a nod he

saw one of the newsmen coming at a plod down the staircase.

"What'll it be, Enrico?" Apple asked as they crossed the empty room to the bar.

"Brandy and soda. But you must let me buy."

"If you insist."

The singer looked at him directly. "Same for you?"

"That'll be fine. Now if you hold the fort I'll nip over to the blower and see if the line's free."

"I'm sure there must be an extension in here."

"And risk being overheard?" Apple asked. He sagged his mouth, incredulous.

"Well . . ."

With a sudden grin: "But you're joking, of course. I'd forgotten that about you, Enrico. I was told you had this great sense of humour."

The opera singer gave a one-sided smile and swayed coyly in that same direction. He bumbled, "Oh, I don't know."

"A real wit, I heard."

"I have my moments, I suppose."

"He has his moments," Apple laughed. "Wow. Some people just have it."

"But you were about to make a call."

"Right on." He strode away from the bar and into the lobby and over to where the reporter sat on the arm of an easy chair. He looked up with tawdry interest on hearing, "I'm Schiller of *Der Spiegel.* What's happening with the English hole-digger?"

"She's denying the story. Claims it's all news to her."

Still in German Apple said, "That can't be true."

"It could be, I think," the reporter said. "But I'll hang around for a while anyway, just in case the lady's playing hard to get."

"Where is she?"

"Up in her room. The other guys're laying siege."

"It's room seventeen, right?"

"Twenty-six and the door's painted green," the newsman said. "Anything else I can help you with?"

"Not immediately," Apple said in turning away. He went to the main door and out into the darkness.

Bearing in mind his own room's number and location Apple strode to the corner, around the side, to the rear. As he went along beside the building's back wall, between it and the parked cars, Apple established, first, that his presence was causing whispers from nearby and, second, that while escape via the lighted window above was plausible, a drainpipe at hand, it wasn't likely to be attempted, never mind accomplished, by a stout woman of sixty.

Not slowing, Apple completed his circuit of the building and arrived back at the entrance, where he slowed to let a pair of tallish men go in ahead of him.

Not until, in the lobby, he saw the two men striding toward the reception desk did Apple realise who they probably were. Only senior policemen, aristocrats and confidence tricksters, he mused, walked with that amount of authority.

Loitering by a framed photograph of a painting of the house next door to Mozart's birthplace, Apple watched the scenario.

The detectives conferred with the manager, who quickly lost his beam and became less pink. Grave with consequence he crossed to the dining room, reappearing after a pause with Jacob Planter, who went to the desk and talked to the men. Next, all three retired to an office behind the desk, ushered there by the manager, who then gave himself a thorough patting and stroking.

Apple hummed his way into the bar.

"Ah, there you are," Enrico Balto said. He was leaning on the counter, glass in hand. "Any luck?"

"Not quite. I got cut off. The operator's working on it. No problem."

"There's your drink. I got you a double."

"Decent of you," Apple said. "I need it." He shot out an eager-seeming hand, which blundered against the glass, which rocked dangerously but might not have fallen over if he hadn't had the presence of mind to act a two-handed saving grab, which did the trick.

Enrico Balto said an oops and the young bartender hurried over to mop up.

"I'm a bag of nerves," Apple said brightly. "Comes from being involved in these high-level operatic matters." And to the barman: "Two more of the same, please."

"Operatic matters," Balto said. "Yes."

"Very much yes. I'd like to explain if I may."

"Do."

Apple said, "As you will have gathered by now, I am an emissary. The name of the opera house has already been mentioned." He did an exaggerated, repeated head-slanting toward the barman in warning against loose talk.

The singer said, "Of course."

Apple doubled over into silent laughter. After making that last as long as he possibly could he weaved himself to near-upright and gasped, "Of course. Hey, that's rich. It's really rich."

Smiling distantly while showing the bottom whites of his eyes the singer said, "Oh well."

"No, really," Apple chuckled. "You're a regular comic. No one would guess it to look at you, you're so grand and stately and everything."

"I have been Pagliacci on more than one occasion."

"It's stayed with you, obviously." He gestured toward the singer's drink like patting a head. "Polish that one off."

Balto had drained his glass by the time two fresh brandies arrived. Of them he said, his eyes swimming in merriment, "Odd that we didn't get served two *spilled* drinks."

Apple heard not even a gist. He was listening to a waterfall sound coming from the dining room. "Quite," he said severely.

Eyes becoming anxious: "Get it?"

Listening hard: "Quite so."

Balto explained, a suggestion of fawn in his manner, "See, when you'd knocked your glass over, you told the barman to . . ."

"Excuse, please," Apple said, moving off. "Must make that call." The waterfall sound he had identified as applause.

Adele Pringle was coming out of the dining room doors, in reverse, bowing, when Apple got there. The people inside were looking this way and still clapping. The women appeared envious, relieved or gratified. The men, faces earnest, were sitting tall as though wanting it to be noted, their tolerance.

The poet butted Apple in the knees with her behind. "Sorry," she said, straightening. She closed the door and turned. "Hello. How was I?"

"Sensational, Pring."

"You don't need to exaggerate."

"I'm not," Apple said. "Listen to that racket." The applause was fading. "It's not often these people get a treat of this highbrow level."

"I dare say that's true," Adele Pringle said. From

the cleavage of her evening gown she brought out a packet of cigarettes.

"Wait a minute. You can't smoke yet."

"Why on earth not?"

Apple drew his upper body back in a performance of pleased astonishment, appreciating with surprise another person's modesty. He overdid it, made his eyes too wide, causing Adele Pringle to ask if anything was wrong.

He said, "Only that you don't seem to realise, Pring, that there has to be an encore. They're waiting for you. They want you. Listen."

Apparently oblivious to the fact of there being nothing to listen to, clapping finished, and unable to see as Apple could that the assembly's attention was everywhere but on herself, the poet said, "It does show how much they appreciated my little reading."

Apple told her, "I was watching their faces all the way through. Rapt, that's the word."

"Really rapt?"

After nodding deeply with sagged eyelids to convey that an affirmative was absurdly unnecessary, Apple took the packet of cigarettes from Adele and popped it back into her cleavage, saying, "You owe your public an encore."

"There is the question of debt, I know."

Apple reached over and opened the door, through which came a barrage of talk. With his hands on her shoulders he turned the poet around and urged her firmly forward.

He murmured, "Give them something nice and long. They've been looking forward to this for days."

"I'll do my best."

The response of the assembly was good to Apple's large signalling for attention behind Adele Pringle's back: at once talk began to lessen. The clapping started equally well in answer to his smiling, nodding, heavy mime of that act, as if he were playing an accordian underwater.

He closed the door and strode away.

"One moment, if you please."

If was the goateed rally official, standing tightly with his evening clothes loose around him.

"No autographs," Apple muttered, still semilost in the world of show-biz.

"I would just like a word."

"Sorry, old man. Can't spare a second."

"Perhaps then we could talk the next time you're outside," the official said nastily. "Spying out the land."

Going on, Apple told him, "Don't think I haven't got my eye on you."

"I don't know what you mean."

Exactly, Apple thought. He went over to the arch and into the bar, where Enrico Balto came toward him with "The joke is, you'd accidentally knocked over your drink, see, and—"

"Yes, where's my drink?" Apple said. "Maybe we ought to get a bottle of champers."

"A celebration?"

"You never can tell. But maybe we'd better wait until I get through."

At the counter Enrico Balto pushed a glass toward Apple, hoisted his own and said, "First let me tell you about that wisecrack of mine."

He did. Listening to the drone but not the words, at its end Apple nodded shrewdly. "Yes," he said.

"Get it?"

More alert, sensing tension, Apple gasped into his laugh routine. He doubled over, slapped the counter,

stamped a foot. "Get it," he whined. "Oh, that's rich.
Get it." He shook his head and showed sorrowing
eyes. "You kill me."

Enrico Balto's lips moved in their reluctant smile-
shape as though he were trying to get to the bottom
of his successful line by repeating it in different tones
and accents and speeds.

Shaking himself, he gave up. "All right," he said,
sergeant to recruits, "that's enough of the humour.
It's time we got down to brass tacks."

Apple, who had been recovering, lurched noisily
back into his act, which, he was convinced, he did
extremely well. Stamping and swaying, it took him
several stammered tries before he could get out a
wheezy "Brass tacks."

"Well, you know, it's an expression."

Apple splurged, "It's an expression, the man says.
He's killing me. He doesn't know his own strength.
God. It's an expression."

Worriedly, Enrico Balto began a long pull on his
brandy. This gave Apple the chance to pick up his
drink and, chuckling weakly between whispers that it
was an expression, meander past the singer in search
of somewhere to empty his glass.

There was, as it happened, a convenient plantpot,
that traditional repository of unwanted drinks; there
was also an inconvenient observer.

Apple saw that he was being watched tight of stare
and grin by the barman, who was patently one of
those people who relish the mirth of others, who hold
themselves in acute readiness for empathetic panting.
He would no more look away than would any other
spectator at an entertainment, especially since this
was free.

"Two more of the same," Apple said.

With his enjoyment on hold, the barman backed off toward the bottles. Apple went close to the counter, swooped low at speed and poured his drink soundlessly onto the floor, rose as quickly and swung backwards from the upright with glass to mouth as though tossing his brandy off in virile style.

The barman shook his head in admiration, which made Apple wish he could do the routine all over again.

He was clopping his mouth appreciatively while turning toward Enrico Balto, who had just drained his drink, when he glanced through the arch and saw Henry Caption. The inventor was crossing the lobby.

"Telephone," Apple said. "Don't go 'way."

Caption looked around as Apple drew alongside. Still walking he said a frosty "That was embarrassing."

"Sneaking out of the reading?"

"Adele's feelings must have been hurt and the others looked daggers at me."

Apple said, "Never mind, Henry. It's all in a beneficial cause. Rewarding."

"What's the reward?"

"Someday you could finish up as a footnote in her biography, if all goes well."

Sounding as though he didn't know whether to be insulted or amused, and if it was the latter hoping he didn't show it, Henry Caption asked, "Whose?"

"The lady you just had to sneak out on."

"This is all very mysterious."

"In here."

It was a small, neglected room, glum as a Sunday parlour. There were two writing tables and a bookcase and a leather armchair. The walls held maps.

After closing the door Apple crossed to the night-backed window. Turning from having drawn the drapes he saw that Henry Caption was looking closely at a map of Austria. He went over, reached out a forefinger to the circled point, asked:

"See how close we are here to the border with the neighbour, Czechoslovakia?"

"If I didn't," the ex-athlete said as he turned, "my eyesight would be in need of attention." He stared up in reproof.

Wondering what had become of that searchlight smile: "What I meant was, I didn't realise how close we were."

"But I wasn't dragged away from a poetry reading to discuss geography, was I?"

"No. I'd like to enlist your help."

Although it appeared as if Henry Caption was about to shake his head, after one swing he held it in the angle of wariness, a bird weighing up the unknown. "Oh?"

"There aren't all that many intelligent people around to whom I can turn."

"Please don't waste your time on flattery."

"I'm not flattering you."

"If I fell for it I wouldn't be overly intelligent, therefore not much use to you."

"Precisely," Apple said. "All I'm doing is stating plain facts. This is a delicate mission and it calls for someone with his wits about him."

Making a gesture, not seeking the time, Henry Caption looked at his watch. "I'll give you a fair hearing," he said. "Please come straight to the point."

"Which is this: Adele Pringle."

"You've already established that."

"So we go on to what happened to her car. You heard? Well, I must tell you that I arranged it."

"You made an anonymous phone call to Customs?"

Apple said, "I certainly did."

The ex-runner took a step backwards. Obviously finding it easier on his neck, the distance, he stepped back again. "I believe you," he said. "Now you'll tell me why."

"Poor Adele has a peculiar health condition. It's rare. Only about one in ten million has it, I'm glad to say, although there are far worse things a person can suffer from."

"What's it called?"

"Aikavolso," Apple said, reading from the map the last half of Czechoslovakia in reverse.

"Never heard of it."

"People keep it to themselves. Its manifestation is in seizures. They're quite awful. And Adele's building up to one, I can tell. That's why I tried to get her removed from the end of the rally."

"I don't see the connexion."

Apple said, "It's the excitement, the thrill of participation. It creates a stress that brings a seizure on. And when it happens, as it's almost sure to, I would like you to assist me in effecting containment."

Being close to the wall, Henry Caption could take only a scuff backwards as he launched into excuses, each interspersed with a meaningful "I hate to say no." He nodded to prove it.

"Fine, fine," Apple kept saying, as well as "I understand perfectly" and "Don't worry, no one's blaming you."

"I really hate to say no."

"Fine, fine."

When Henry Caption, nodding, had fallen silent,

Apple said reassuringly, "It's not a matter of life or death. Adele isn't even going to injure herself. So, if you can't help, she'll have to go through with it."

Nodding: "Yes."

Sighing: "I just hate to see a woman make a spectacle of herself, that's all. I hate to see her threshing about. And all those lewd gestures. It's so pathetic."

Suddenly gaunt, Henry Caption whispered, "Okay." He spoke as softly as though wanting to go unheard.

Apple, who had no more been aware of his dejected stance than he had of how much he was enjoying his role, asked an invalid's querulous "What's that?"

In a loud snap: "I said very well, I'll help."

The change in mood brought Apple upright and alert. When his tinge of regret had faded he rubbed his hands together. It was a comfort, as was his poignant "Thank you."

Impatiently: "What do I do?"

Brisk, fearing that if he didn't get on with it the ex-athlete might change his mind, Apple said, "The mo ment she falls we have to move into action. I'll take care of her feet. Reflexology is pretty complex but I know the field inside out. Your department is from the chin up, more or less. It's fairly straightforward."

Uneasily: "It is?"

"Simple as one two three."

"Will there be frothing and stuff?"

"No no. I'll only need to give you one lesson and you'll have it pat. Turn around, please."

Henry Caption obliged. Deadly serious, worried about failing at a procedure which he had brought off only once before, under ideal conditions and with a willing subject, Apple lifted finger-flexing hands and placed them on Caption's neck. His thumbs found the right pulse-points. He began to apply pressure, in a quiet drone the while explaining the operation.

Within seconds, blood kept from his brain, Henry Caption was starting to sag. When asked if he understood he answered with a dreamy "Mmm?" Apple increased the pressure until the only thing holding Caption upright was the grip on his neck.

With the ex-runner stretched out unconscious on the floor, Apple went swiftly through his pockets. He found no room-key. His own room would have to do.

The job of getting Henry Caption up far enough to enable Apple, on his knees, to do the fireman's lift was so farcical a performance of slithery torso and flopping arms that Apple thought of something else.

He was still wondering if he should get a new collar for Monico, his dog, and if so what colour, when he finally got the dead weight in place on his shoulder. He rose with creaky thighs.

Out of the room Apple stumped across the lobby, getting from the reporter a stare of interest, from the manager fast attendance.

The latter joined Apple as he was thudding onto the stairs. "What's wrong?"

Apple explained about Henry Caption's Aikavolso. "Could you get the key to his room, please?"

"I have a pass-key."

They went on up.

Blue was perfectly acceptable for a collar, Apple agreed busily, which helped him to not notice how crippling he was finding his burden and to not dwell on its suddenly becoming conscious.

In the room Apple dropped Henry Caption onto his bed, where he bounced. The manager he got rid of with pushes and gasps, both genuine, the one born of urgency, the other of his struggle for even breathing. Door closed, he untied and pulled off his bow-tie.

Its length sufficed. With one end tied to Caption's shoelaces, still in their shoes, and the other end securing his wrists, at the rear, the trussing job was done.

Henry Caption was stirring as Apple drew him carefully down onto the floor. He slid him under the bed with his front to the wall, a position his trussing would keep him in unless he got out from under, which Apple made improbable by lying at the bedside, after arranging bedclothes as hangings, the wardrobe and a chest of drawers and an armchair. The bedclothes would help deaden shouts. A final touch was hooking on the outside doorknob a Do Not Disturb sign.

Fit again, Apple went to the stairs and started down. He slowed, seeing at the bottom a barrier in the shape of the rally official, who stood on the last step with his arms extremely folded.

This would have been fine with Apple if it weren't for the fact that, as he stopped three steps up, he saw through the bar arch that Enrico Balto looked to be on the point of leaving. He had that sway about him.

"There's something odd going on with you," the official accused. He spoke in the tone that often went with narrowed eyes.

"You'll have to excuse me."

"Oh no I won't, Porter. I'm staying here until I get to the bottom of this."

"After all," Apple said, "you have your duty to the others to think of." He made to go past at one side, was blocked by the official, added, "You're not one to take your responsibilities lightly."

"You must understand, Porter, that I have a certain duty to the other members."

"I do, yes."

"I don't take responsibility as lightly as others might, you know."

"I should hope not."

The official said, "Therefore I'd like to know why you lied about that time you were naked."

"I? Tell a lie?"

"Yes, Porter, in essence. You failed to mention Prunella Bank's part in that affair."

Enrico Balto dawdled toward the bar arch, Apple saw. He said, "One tries to keep a lady's name out of these unpalatable matters."

"Of course," the official said cynically. "To be sure."

"I can see you're a man of the world."

"And not a blind one."

"Well, it's been lovely," Apple said. "But I really must be running along."

"Oh no you don't, Porter. There's also the strange business of the goldfish."

"Are you confessing?"

The official unfolded his arms threateningly. "Never mind the clever stuff."

Enrico Balto passed through the archway, gazed thoughtfully down. "Must go," Apple said. Although he could have broken the little man in two with a sneeze, he knew, the most he could bring himself to do was barge forward. He and the official thunked together.

Applause sounded from the dining room. Through its glass doors could be seen Adele Pringle coming in reverse, bowing. Enrico Balto was heading for the exit.

The official had hold of Apple's silken lapels. He

said, "You've evaded the issue long enough, Porter. I'm sick of it."

"So am I," Apple said. Taking the man by his elbows he lifted him in the air. He lifted until they were face to face, almost touching noses, when he said murmurously, "If you do not depart in peace I shall hurl you against that wall."

Quietly but pugnaciously: "I dare you."

A voice called out, "Yoo hoo, Enrico!"

It was Adele Pringle. Having come out of the dining room, where applause still rippled, she was waving at Enrico Balto, who had been about to go outdoors.

He turned. "Yes?"

"You're on, dear."

Nodding, the singer went toward her. "Thank you."

Adele said, "I'm going to come in and listen as well."

"Naturally."

When the performers had gone into the dining room, Apple and the man he was holding up stopped watching and turned their faces back nose to nose.

The official said, "I don't want to miss this."

"Neither do I," Apple said. "I'll tell you about my investigations later."

"Oh?"

"I've been trying not to get others involved."

"I see."

Apple put him down. "You're no chicken, however. I can see that now. I'll be able to rely on you when the gore starts to flow.

"Ah."

"Go on in. Save a place for me."

Face tight, clothes looking looser than before, the

official hurried off. He was followed by the reporter and the manager into the dining room, where someone was pounding out an intro on the piano.

Apple sauntered over to reception, humming to show the total desertion he was not up to no good. What up to he was, in general, formed another matter, though had he faced the question he would at least have been able to state that, for the time being, all the Possibles were under his control. He hoped.

With a glance toward the dining room to make sure he had no observers, Apple went behind the reception desk. To stay unobserved he crouched down on reaching the office door, which position also helped him eavesdrop.

As Apple knew, much of the seventy per cent of a person's energy which he uses simply to stand upright can be applied to the listening effort.

The voices were clear. One of the policemen was asking questions, politely and in excellent English; Jacob Planter was stonewalling arrogantly, claiming to not understand the questions in a way that would have convinced any intelligent jury of his guilt.

Soothed by the feeling of power bestowed by being illicitly privy to other people's talk or letters or acts, Apple stayed on beside the door. Only once did his attention stray, although he wasn't fully conscious of the fact, didn't understand that when he clenched his toes it was to assist Enrico Balto in hitting a high note.

Sated, Apple rose. In moving away he noticed the bank of pigeonholes. Accepting immediately that he had come here for this, he got Henry Caption's key, which he twirled boldly as he crossed to the staircase.

Above, he again listened at a door. He heard growls

and swearing, the latter poor on invention. Disinterested, he locked the door and headed for an upper floor.

Peering with slow caution around the last corner Apple saw half a dozen men. Sitting or lounging near the door of Mavis Whittington's room, they were discussing natural phenomena: why the bottle of whiskey took longer to pass around now that it was close to being empty.

Apple retreated. Yes, he mused in facing the question he hadn't faced before, all under control.

He went downstairs.

Leaning on the wall by the dining room doors, after a look inside the check presences and to win the bet with himself that the rally official would be wedged somewhere with no place saved for anyone else, Apple listened to Enrico Balto's final piece.

The applause was still lingering when the door opened. The third person to come out was Prunella. "Hello," she said from behind her gauze. "Did you hear? He's got a great voice."

She was followed by other people, including Adele Pringle and the singer himself. Everyone was talking. Someone asked Prunella if there wasn't something she could do to entertain while she was telling Apple she intended taking a turn outside before going to bed. Someone else implored Enrico Balto for an encore while he, shaking his hair emphatically, was telling Apple they had to get together on the La Scala thing. A third someone was asking Adele for her autograph while she was telling Apple he would be perfect.

He got around to asking, "For what?"

"The game, dear."

Then there were three women in front of him.

They shunted him sideways, they backed him into the dining room, they escorted him by force over to where tables were being moved to create a space.

Loudly they cried, "Mr. Porter's on our side!"

Unnerved, his scalp prickling, Apple found himself in the centre of an agreeing/complaining mob. Wonderful, some called in respect of his being on a particular side. Terrible, others shouted.

With people snapping Fair and Unfair at each other Apple said in a reasonable tone that he wasn't playing. No one took any notice, and when he tried to draw away more people joined in the holding.

An Unfair yelled, "At least he should have his shoes off." Two of the Fairs, rocking their heads indulgently, squatted by Apple's feet, which he then began shuffling to foil attempts to unfasten his laces.

"Unfair," he called.

"Fair," people shouted.

Apple as well as shuffling was looking around for an escape and telling any face that happened to be directed toward him that he couldn't play much as he would love to because of that stupid old back trouble of his. Yes, you're perfect, the faces said.

On seeing that none of the Possibles were present Apple redoubled his efforts to get free. He went stumbling and lurching among the crowd with shouts of "Unfair unfair."

Some shouted the same and some the opposite and some laughed at his tomfoolery, his party spirit.

The situation became nightmarish.

Apple told himself both that it was retribution for all his transgressions against innocent ralliers and a plot arranged by the one who wasn't innocent.

He struggled on. Somebody was down there holding onto one leg like an orphan while the other was bcing hit behind the knee in a try at making him lift his foot for shoe-removal.

Apple had the terrifying suspicion that if he fell down all would be lost.

A clanging sounded.

Looking around wild-eyed and unkempt, draped in people, Apple saw Jacob Planter come striding into the dining room. The inventor had a hand-bell. His vigorous, stern ringing cut into the chaos and reduced it by half.

Pushing without ceremony through the people, Jacob Planter reached Apple's side. Roughly, after handing his bell to someone, he pulled him loose of the holders.

He barked, "This man is needed."

Apple whispered, "What?"

Turning, knocking a woman aside, Planter towed Apple off toward the glass doors. When they got there, free of followers, he looked behind with "Step lively. No time to be lost."

SEVEN

They left the hotel by the main door, stepping out into the night with Jacob Planter again urging haste. The moon, still free of clouds, looked close enough to hit with a newspaper.

Apple asked, "Where we going?"

"For a fast drive."

The answer was of no more consequence to Apple than had been the question, which he had asked only to show himself how fast he was returning to normal. He had returned when the other man spoke again, as they were circling the building.

"Where's your tie, Porter?"

"I used it to truss someone up."

"Very funny."

As they neared the hotel's rear the clutch of cars came in sight. From somewhere in it shrilled a whistle, which was answered by another.

Jacob Planter said, "We're using your car, obviously."

"What's so obvious about it?"

"I wouldn't have saved you from your playmates otherwise. Where is it?"

"This way," Apple said, moving in front. "What's happening?"

"Explain later. It's an emergency."

From above the nearest vehicle a head appeared,

showing clearly in the moonlight. A voice challenged, "Who goes there?"

"None of your damn business," the inventor said, sneery, while Apple answered that they were planning to take his car out, if that was all right.

Sulky: "Just doing my job. There's a thief about."

Jacob Planter said, "Then tell the police. There's a couple of 'em in the bar."

They went on, threading their way to Ethel, who had a coating of dew. After two minutes of impatient hissing by Planter they were in and on the move, Ethel coughing as she jerkily went because of her usual desire to stand still until she got warm.

Over his shoulder Apple said, "I didn't see you at the poetry reading, nor at Balto's recital."

The inventor, on the folding seat, asked, "Are you trying to make conversation?"

"Only being a good host. Forget it. You can't stand poetry and you're tone-deaf."

"Neither one. I was occupied with those two cop pers I mentioned back there."

"*You* were?"

Jacob Planter didn't respond until Ethel, warm now, was out on the road and building up speed. He said, "They were under the impression, it finally came out, that I was involved in this country with industrial espionage."

"That's interesting."

"Glad you think so."

"Is it true?"

"You're a regular clown, Porter."

"Thanks," Apple said. "So it isn't true and you were able to convince them of that."

The inventor said, "They had no evidence. What

had brought them to me was an anonymous phone call."

"I've had my share of that lark."

"Did it make you vengeful?"

"No, just pissed off."

"I'll believe anything," Jacob Planter said. "Can't this wagon go any faster?"

Apple said, "You must have a very short memory." He put his foot down on the accelerator.

As Ethel began to shimmy, the inventor moved back onto the full seat. He called, "That's a bit more like it. As long as she holds together."

Apple decided that, instead of pursuing the tit-for-tat with a crack about people who drove blindly into weeds, which wouldn't be all that clever anyway, it was time he weighed up the situation.

But all he knew was that he instinctively felt himself to be heading in the right direction, even though logic told him that Jacob Planter could be an accomplice of Defector and could be taking naïve Agent One on a chase after a wild goose. Planter, in fact, was not all that he seemed.

Apple sent Ethel speeding forward. They had already crossed one highway and were now speeding along another among cars, the direction indicated by the passenger, who was sitting tense and upright as he watched the way ahead.

Not for the first time during his years of ownership Apple wished there were a seat beside him instead of the open luggage area. He could engage Planter in talk and hopefully worm out of him what his game was.

However, the notion of committing such a sacrilege to Ethel made Apple, as always before, take the wish back and pretend he had never had it in the first place.

After they had sped along for another five minutes in silence Jacob Planter said, "Turn at that tree."

The huge pine stood stark in the headlights. Apple made the turn, leaving behind the highway and its traffic. Or most of it; for as he went on along the narrow, rough road he saw headlights appear in the rear distance.

"You know," he said chattily over his shoulder, "we may have someone following us."

"That doesn't matter."

"Now I come to think of it, the car could have been there right from the beginning."

"Forget it, Porter. There's no reason why it should be on our tail."

"No reason why it shouldn't, either."

"Maybe you're paranoid about such things," Jacob Planter said. "I'm not."

"I watch television a lot."

"Just watch the road and keep your foot down."

Not bothering to ask Planter why he thought his orders would be obeyed, Apple slowed slightly, which he hoped would be unnoticeable to his passenger.

Gradually, the car behind drew closer. Despite the full moon and clear sky, behind its headlights the vehicle was unseeable. Apple, however, was able to judge it as being low-slung.

Jacob Planter asked, "What's the matter?"

"Nothing. This is a tricky bit of road."

"I don't suppose these old springs can stand much abuse."

Rather than be conned into speed Apple said,

"You're right." He continued as before. But the car behind had also slowed. This he reported.

Planter said, "Tomorrow see a shrink."

The road worsened when they passed around a bend. The surroundings also changed, from fields to woodland, the trees encroaching right up to the roadside. It was like driving through a tunnel. The car behind maintained its position.

There was something definitely familiar to Apple about the set of those headlights. Since the chance was excellent of the car being a tail and not a casual, he knew he would have to settle the matter.

"Watch out!" he yelled, after which he braked hard. Jacob Planter was thrown forward onto the floor.

The car behind, slower in stopping than Ethel, was illuminated slightly by its headlights being reflected from the trees. Through his rear-view mirror Apple could just make out the form as that of an MG.

"What the hell?" the passenger snarled.

"Sorry," Apple said, taking Ethel forward. "I nearly hit a rabbit."

"Jesus. A rabbit."

"It's bad luck to hit rabbits and white cats."

Jacob Planter was standing in a stoop. "Spare me your superstitions," he said. "You can stop soon."

"Yes, sir. At your service, sir."

"Turn left at that fork."

"Certainly, sir," Apple said. "What happens if the car behind follows us?"

"Make your own guesses," Planter said. "Turn."

Swinging the steering-wheel Apple forked onto a dirt track. Although the trees were younger and less close at hand they seemed a threat as Ethel's headlights swept them up and down in her rocking on the track's wavy surface.

The MG was coming behind.

Jacob Planter said, "All right, Porter." He was holding on at each side to keep himself up on his feet. "You can stop right there."

With ample room beside the track Apple, slowing, steered carefully off. He brought Ethel to a stop. At once his passenger opened the door and got out. He set off into the trees.

Apple alighted. Bravely leaving his headlights on and the doors unlocked he followed Planter at a fast lope. With glances to the side he saw the MG come to a halt.

"See?" he said.

The man in front answered that he wasn't blind. He went on striding through the trees, his way visible in the moonlight. Apple tailed on at a slower speed. He kept looking back.

A figure had left the sports car and was coming this way. Tree trunks made the establishing of details difficult, but Apple had the impression that he was seeing a female.

Jacob Planter stumbled, cursed, went on. Apple followed at his own pace, which proved to be slower than that of the other follower, who loomed closer.

She was definitely female. Apple could see a dress, long hair, a pale face.

The sounds of passage ahead ended. Looking around from another stare at the woman, Apple saw that Jacob Planter had come to a stop. He was near a link fence. Eight feet high, topped with barbed wire, it stretched off into the trees in either direction.

Planter sank down on one knee and started fiddling with a shoe. He hummed a tune.

Apple looked the other way. He called, "Hello there."

"Hello," a voice said. It belonged to Prunella Bank. "Is everything all right?"

"I think so."

Prunella stopped. After gazing all around she asked, "Sure?"

"Perfectly," Apple said. "Where's your bandages and dark glasses and stuff?"

"Took 'em off as I drove. They were being out-drama'd."

Apple turned the other way. Jacob Planter, back on his feet again, was holding what looked like a pistol. Apple said, "That's not a gun, I hope."

"It better be."

"Now wait a minute."

"Yes," Prunella said, "do."

Lifting the gun high above his head, aiming at the sky, Jacob Planter fired. Apple flinched. He flinched again as Planter fired a second time, and asked, "How long does this go on?"

"Finished," the other man said. After pocketing his gun he stepped close to the fence and with hardly any pause, and with no more trouble than climbing a ladder, went right to the top. He flipped over the barbed wire, dropped, landed neatly with his feet together.

He murmured, "Well done, sir."

Impressed, Apple asked, "How'd you do that?"

"Gadgets on the front of my shoes," Planter said. "After all, I am an inventor."

From behind him, far away, lights appeared, not as glints through trees but moving glows in the sky. At the same time, from the same source, came the barking of dogs and the curt shouts of men.

"I like searchlights," Jacob Planter said following a glance back. He smiled. "Now I can relax. My nerves have been making me quite irritable."

"So I noticed."

"Good. You're altogether a good witness. You too, Pru. Nice to have you around."

"Thank you, Jake," Prunella said, coming closer. "What're you doing?"

"Defecting."

"That's rather silly."

"Not at all."

"I hope you've thought it over carefully."

"Only for about ten years," the inventor said. "But what're you doing? Here, I mean."

"Well," Prunella said, "I was sitting in the MG when Ethel zipped off. I thought someone had pinched her. So I switched off the shriek alarm and followed."

"Terrific," Apple said, impressed again.

"Then when you got out I recognised you."

"You should've spoken up."

"I thought you might be doing something odd."

Apple asked, "Why were you sitting in the MG?"

"The guards told me they'd just chased away a man who'd been trying to break into one of the cars."

"That was me," Jacob Planter said cheerfully.

"So I went to keep an eye on the MG for a while."

Planter: "And for my part, I went to con Apple into driving me out here."

"Yes, I thought that's what you were up to," Apple lied, drawling. He rubbed his hands together to weaken the imagined scene wherein Angus Watkin was asking how Defector had got to the border and Apple was saying, "I drove him there."

The man on the other side of the fence told him, "By the way, sorry about the bits of sabotage I played on you. It was nothing personal."

"Thank you."

"I thought you could possibly be a British secret agent who was onto me and who'd be a problem."

Apple acted delight. "Really? A secret agent?"

"I found out you weren't when I acted anger and threw a punch at you. Sorry about that as well, old man. The accident with the Cord was my own fault, of course. But I wanted to see how you'd react to attack. You did so like an amateur."

While Prunella was telling Jacob Planter to send her a postcard if he was quite, quite sure he wanted to do this silly thing, and Planter was congratulating Prunella on being so . . . so . . . ("Intrepid," she tossed in), Apple was seeing what the instructor had meant that day at Damian House.

After failing for the seventh time to get his tall pupil to do the judo throw right, he had sighed, "Never mind, Porter. Sometimes it pays to be useless."

Which, Apple reminded himself, though his cover was unblown, didn't alter the fact that he hadn't prevented the defection. But then, neither had anyone else, including DG7.

"Good-bye," Jacob Planter said. "Good-bye." With a jaunty wave he turned and walked off toward where the barks and shouts were growing louder.

"Good-bye," Apple and Prunella chorused. They moved together, put an arm around each other, set off for the track at an amble.

Prunella tapped his shoulder with her head, saying, "Tell me it's not true what Jake said."

"Mmm?"

"Tell me you're a valiant secret agent who constantly risks his life and who's as hard as nails and who sweeps women off their feet."

"Consider yourself told."

"Thank you, I shall."

Apple smiled, musing:

It is moonlight. Agent One is on foreign soil, among the trees of a forest. There are searchlights and snarling dogs and armed soldiers. Nearby is a man with a gun and in the air lingers the cruel stench of gunfire. There is a beautiful woman. Ethel is waiting. Agent One is wearing a tuxedo and he has no tie on.

He had no tie on with his tuxedo, Apple reflected again as Prunella said, "You have failed in your latest perilous mission, alas. But then, you can't win 'em all."

Tightening his arm around her shoulders, Apple said, "Oh?"

Marc Lovell is the author of twelve previous Appleton Porter novels, including *The Spy Who Fell Off the Back of a Bus* and *That Great Big Trenchcoat in the Sky*. *Apple Spy in the Sky* was made into the film *Trouble with Spies*. Mr. Lovell has lived for nearly thirty years on the island of Majorca.